# Faith, Hope, Love & Luck:

## A Collection Of Stories For St. Patrick's Day

# Faith, Hope, Love & Luck:

## A Collection Of Stories
## For St. Patrick's Day

From the Editors
Of *True Story* And
*True Confessions*

Published by True Renditions, LLC


True Renditions, LLC
105 E. 34th Street, Suite 141
New York, NY 10016

ISBN: 978-1-938877-88-9

Visit us on the web at www.truerenditionsllc.com.

# Contents

# JUST MY LUCK
## My Sister Wanted The Man I Love,
## But I Can't Give Him Up!

St. Patrick's Day used to be my very favorite day of the year. Better than my birthday or Valentine's Day. Even better than Christmas.

I couldn't have been more than four or five when Grandma swept my long red hair into a neat ponytail, helped me wash my hands like a surgeon, put a big white apron over my head, and tied it behind my waist.

My first job was to poke cloves into a huge white onion and carefully peel carrots, while Grandma peeled potatoes and carefully trimmed bits of fat off the corned beef brisket. Before long, her biggest pot was simmering on the stove. She threw in spices from the cupboard, parsley from the window box garden. She said she'd add the cabbage after four hours. Plenty of time to bake shamrock cookies. Grandma made the dough, helped me use the cookie cutter to make shamrocks, carefully spaced them on cookie sheets, and let me sprinkle green sugar over the tops before they went into the oven.

Grandma surprised me with the bright green dress she'd sewn for me, and helped me tie a matching ribbon in my hair.

There wasn't an empty seat to be found around the huge dining room table when it was time to slice the corned beef and serve it with the potatoes and carrots. Mom hurried in the door just as we were about to sit down, and apologized for being late. Kelly and I just smiled. Mom was always late. All of the aunts and uncles were there. All of the cousins, too. Nobody had to explain what it meant to have the luck of the Irish. I knew lucky was being surrounded by so much happiness and love.

St. Patrick's Day stopped being my favorite day of the year when I turned sixteen. Two months after Grandma died, I tried ever so hard to make corned beef and cabbage in her biggest pot, but it didn't smell nearly as wonderful as Grandma's. If only I'd paid closer attention to the spices she'd added. Was it a pinch of thyme or two? What else had she added?

The phone rang all day long. Uncle Joe said he had a bad case of the sniffles. One set of cousins said they had spring finals to study for. Another apologized for making other plans. With a dozen different excuses, the rest of the family made it clear they weren't going to

1

come all the way across town to cram into Mom's cramped condo. My big sister, Kelly, and Mom politely tasted the corned beef and cabbage I'd worked so hard on. Then, we ate every last crumb of six-dozen shamrock cookies. At least, the cookies turned out as good as Grandma's.

I'd learned a lot working with Grandma in her kitchen. I probably could have figured out just what spices she'd used to make her corned beef and cabbage so special by experimenting again and again, but my heart just wasn't up to the task. It didn't seem to matter. Nothing seemed to matter with her gone.

So much more than just the nice silver-haired lady who took me to school and picked me up afterwards while Mom worked long hours at a downtown law office; Grandma was the special person who listened to all my secret hopes and dreams, made me believe I could make them come true if I studied hard enough, and worked hard enough.

It was almost impossible to force myself out of bed each morning, knowing she wouldn't be there to brighten the day better than the brightest sun.

My big sister had the perfect answer. Even though she never spent more than a dollar or two to buy me a card for my birthday or Christmas, she took me to the fancy beauty shop where she spent a fortune to get her hair cut. When we walked out of that elegant place, I couldn't believe what I saw in the wall of mirrors. My twenty-one old sister, and I, could have almost passed for twins!

I should have guessed Kelly had more on her mind than just seeing her baby sister smile, again. We weren't back at the house five minutes before she told me about her really hot date with a dealer from the Indian casino where she worked.

"If I blow him off, he'll never ask again. I couldn't find a soul to cover for me. Erin, you have to pretend to be me."

All afternoon long, Kelly drilled me until I knew exactly what to do so nobody figured out our big secret. She taught me how to flash her ID badge at the computer screen to log in and out, how to place drink orders at the bar, how to properly serve drinks.

"Some customers will tip you in cash. Others will give you chips." Kelly carefully explained which chips were worth one dollar, five dollars, twenty-five dollars, even a hundred dollars. "Don't think you'll see any of those, Erin. We'll split the tips fifty-fifty. I'll bet your share winds up being more than you could earn in a month baby-sitting!"

"But you have to be twenty-one to work at the casino!"

"I am twenty-one."

"I'm not."

"By the time I finish with your makeup, you and I are gonna be the

2

only ones who know that." Makeup wasn't all Kelly did to make me look older. She dug around in her drawer until she found the padded push-up bra she'd worn until she blossomed. "You'll need this, so my uniform doesn't look like a baggy clown suit on you."

"If Mom ever finds out—"

"She's working late all month. Some sort of special project for her boss. Just leave her a note saying you're spending the night at a friend's house, and make sure the friend knows to cover for you in case Mom calls to check up on you."

When I took my first step into the casino, I thought this must be what heaven was like. It was the closest thing to perfect I'd ever seen. Bright lights. Beautiful colors. Slot machines making people squeal with excitement as they hit the jackpot.

Heaven was the last thing on my mind after I'd been there long enough to log in and start serving drinks. It was hard enough to keep my balance on Kelly's hooker high heels without somebody bumping into me every couple of minutes. My eyes stung from the cigarette smoke, and my throat felt like it was on fire.

Kelly was right about one thing: most of the customers tipped generously. Getting shoved around and breathing all that smoke wasn't any worse than changing poopy diapers and chasing toddlers. If the first few hours were a good indication of how the whole shift would go, then it paid a lot better, too. My sister had been wrong about one thing. A guy who looked just like Uncle Joe  gave me a hundred-dollar chip. Actually, he gave me two. He wanted me to help him out to his car.

"Had a little too much to drink, sugar."

"Yessir." The customer is always right. Almost right. This jerk had much too much to drink to walk a straight line. No way was I going to help him get behind the wheel and drive away so he could kill somebody. I looked around, hoping to see one of the uniformed security guards that I'd been so afraid might figure out I wasn't my sister when I first walked in. No such luck.

"Need a little help?"

At first, I didn't see any clue that the handsome man with just a hint of silver in his chocolate brown hair worked for the casino. Then, I noticed the cord behind his ear that obviously wasn't a hearing aid and the subtle gold nameplate on his pocket. Hugh Murtagh, director of security, promised to call a cab for the drunk, and invited me to grab a hamburger when we were done for the night.

Mom was so strict that I'd never been on a date with guys my own age. I was allowed to go to the movies or to the mall with a group of kids. Nothing more than that until I turned seventeen. "It's what's best for you, Erin. I want you to be safe."

3

Mom would have gone ballistic if she ever found out how far from safe I was in this place. I had to be a juggler to figure out how to balance the tall and short glasses on the heavy drink tray and still manage to keep a hand free to grab the tip, a too-friendly customer tried to shove into my bra, or some other place strange hands didn't belong.

"Just smile, Erin. Keep smiling."

Wasn't that what Kelly had instructed me to do?

The only time I really felt like smiling was when the shift was finally over, and it was time for "Kelly" to log out for the night. My feet were killing me. I couldn't wait to get to the car and trade the killer heels for some sneakers. I was much too tired to remember that I'd planned to use part of my share of the tip money to play a slot machine after I was officially off duty. I'd forgotten something much more important, too.

Hugh Murtagh was waiting for me at the door. I almost made some sort of lame excuse to get out of the hamburger date I'd forgotten in the blur of activity after Hugh took care of the drunk. Almost. I wasn't quite tired enough to pass up the once in a lifetime opportunity to sit across from those deep dark chocolate eyes, and pretend I was old enough to be on a real date with this handsome man.

I was embarrassed when he escorted me to the boring beige secondhand clunker that was all I could afford—even after Mom chipped in some money to supplement what I'd earned baby-sitting. If only Kelly had lent me her shiny red sports car.

Hugh didn't seem to notice what I was driving. He kept looking at me like I was the most beautiful girl, most beautiful woman—he'd ever seen.

"My pickup is parked in the next lot. You can drop me there, and then follow me to the restaurant."

I'd never been to Benny's Burger Barn. The huge place really did look like a barn. There was loud country/western music blaring when we walked in, but Hugh led me toward a quiet area with bright red booths.

"How do you like your burger?"

"Medium rare with everything on it. On second thought, hold the onions."

"Don't do that on my account. I'm getting double onions on mine!"

"Do they have onion rings?"

"Only the best in the town and curly fries, too."

"My favorite. Makes it hard to decide."

"Not hard at all. We'll get an order of each."

Thank goodness, it was after hours. Kelly had given me her casino ID, but kept her driver's license. No way did I want to risk ordering a drink and getting carded.

4

Root beer in an icy mug washed away the smoky taste in my throat. Hugh told me he'd started working at the Indian casino just after he got out of the Army.

"Traded one uniform for another. I'd spent some time working with the military police so that stood out on my resume. Good thing, too, because the Indian casinos give preference to Native American applicants. Probably never would have moved up to this position if I hadn't met and married Raven."

Those deep chocolate eyes looked so sad as Hugh told me about falling in love with the beautiful Indian blackjack dealer, managing to convince her family and his that it was truly love, and not just lust they felt for each other.

"We were married for seven years before Raven got pregnant. I think we'd both kind of given up on the idea of having a baby. It was like we'd hit the biggest jackpot in the world when the doctor said her 'horrible case of the flu' would be born in six months. Everything seemed to be going fine until her eighth month. Losing her and the baby was even harder than killing an enemy soldier."

I tried to find just the right words to pry Hugh away from his painful past, help him see there was a bright future to look forward to. I must have managed to come close to saying the right thing. He reached across the table to ever so gently grab my hand.

If the food hadn't arrived at just that moment, I probably would have done something really stupid like lean over and kiss him.

No steak could have tasted any better than the perfectly grilled burger, onion rings, and curly fries.

Even though I was too stuffed to even think about ordering dessert, I agreed to split a piece of frozen mud pie, just to have an excuse to spend a few more minutes with Hugh.

A few more minutes weren't nearly enough. I wanted to spend the night with him, and yearned to spend the rest of my life with this wonderful man.

No such luck. He walked me back to my car, gave me an Uncle Joe peck on the cheek, and asked if I wanted him to follow me home to make sure I got there, safely.

"No, thanks; I'll be fine. Thank you for tonight."

"It was just a burger. Now, if there were a restaurant that served corned beef and cabbage like my mother used to make— "

Without thinking, I invited him to dinner after church on Sunday.

"My Grandma used to make wonderful corned beef and cabbage. Are you willing to gamble that I can come close to hers and your mother's?"

"Sounds like a safe bet. See you at work tomorrow, or should I say later today?"

5

I was floating on air, dreaming all sorts of wonderful dreams, after the exquisite time we'd spent together when Hugh's words suddenly landed me back on earth with a sickening thud. Hugh Murtagh, director of security, wouldn't see me at the casino; he'd see Kelly!

It was so hard to concentrate on the road as I drove home. I had to figure out some way to make the impossible happen, some way to keep Hugh from learning I was just a sixteen-year-old kid, instead of a woman who could heal his broken heart.

I wasn't the least bit tired. Parking where I could see Mom leave for work but she couldn't see me, I turned the radio on low and waited until she drove away before I drove into the garage and went inside.

Kelly's bloodshot eyes told me she hadn't gotten home much before I did. I put the night's tips on the table, couldn't help but feel more than a little bit proud when she gasped at the two hundred-dollar chips.

"Did everything go okay?"

"More than just okay. I met the most incredible man, but he thinks I'm you. He expects to see me at the casino later, but it will be you, and I invited him to dinner Sunday. It's just all messed up."

"Slow down, Erin. Who is Mr. Wonderful? Customer or casino employee?"

"He's the Director of Security."

"Well, isn't that just too freakin' perfect? He'd get me fired in a heartbeat if he found out what we did."

"Maybe if we explained. . . ."

"Look, I'll just pretend that something's come up—some sort of family emergency—and then just sort of forget to invite him for a different night."

"No. He's really nice. All he wants is some of Grandma's corned beef and cabbage—"

"Which you don't know how to make; remember?"

"I'm pretty sure I know what I did wrong. Couldn't we just pretend one more time? I'll be the kid sister, and you'll be you, except you'll pretend you cooked the magnificent dinner, and you'll be you extra nice to Hugh?"

And then, you'll disappear off the face of the earth, so I can pretend to be you and live happily ever after with Hugh? Of course, I didn't say the words out loud; but I sure wished hard that some miracle like that could happen. Mom said there was no such thing as love at first sight, but I was sure I'd met my soul mate while I was pretending to be Kelly. No! Hugh was much too mature to ever be able to fall in love with a kid like me.

Maybe the only realistic scenario was for him to marry Kelly. She obviously needed somebody more stable than the guys she was usually attracted to—every bit as much as Hugh needed somebody to help him recover from the pain of losing Raven and his baby, needed somebody to make him feel loved and happy again. If I tried really hard, maybe I could force myself to be happy for them, and settle for being Auntie Erin to their beautiful babies. Maybe.

Kelly slammed the door on her way out. I didn't have a clue whether I needed to shop for Sunday dinner or just hope she'd let Hugh down, gently.

Even though I hadn't been the least bit tired the night before, my long hours pretending to be my sister caught up to me somewhere in the middle of my history homework. I fell asleep long before Kelly got home from the casino. She shook me till I woke up.

"Hugh was so excited about Sunday that I didn't have the heart to disappoint him. You better get busy, little sister. He's expecting a really special dinner."

And that's exactly what he got. I could almost feel Grandma's hands guiding mine as I filled her biggest pot and set it on the stove to simmer. Not a moment of hesitation. I suddenly knew exactly which spices to reach for in the cupboard, and I somehow sensed exactly how much I should add. I'd planted parsley in the patio garden, so I harvested two handfuls to chop and toss in. I baked a lemon bundt cake for dessert, and set the table with Grandma's best china.

I could tell Mom really liked Hugh, but it was a cinch all that would have changed in a heartbeat if she knew I was the one who loved him instead of Kelly.

Hugh seemed so relaxed, almost as though he'd sat at our table for dozens of Sundays.

"This is the best corned beef and cabbage I've had since my mother made it for me!"

I had to gently kick Kelly under the table to remind her to thank him for the compliment. Mom looked a bit confused, but then smiled as though she'd figured out Kelly's little white lie to impress her new significant other.

Kelly and Hugh took a walk to get frozen yogurt to go with the cake while Mom and I cleared the table and made a pot of coffee. They must have argued about something because Hugh didn't look the least bit relaxed when they got back.

He politely finished dessert and offered to dry the dishes. Surely, Kelly would put on rubber gloves to protect her expensive manicure and do the washing. She wouldn't leave me alone in the kitchen with him. She couldn't! She did.

I was so nervous that I was sure I'd drop Grandma's best china. How could I be this close to Hugh, and not let it slip that I loved him and wanted to spend the rest of my life with him? It didn't matter that I was young enough to be his daughter. It didn't matter that I'd pretended to be Kelly. All that mattered was that we belonged together. We were soul mates, destined to spend eternity in each other's arms.

I could almost see Grandma's special smile when I finally worked up my nerve to tell the truth. Hugh didn't look the least bit surprised when I spilled my guts.

"Kiddo, I figured it out the minute I walked through the door and met Kelly's little sister. Hell, I should have figured it out that night at the casino. Your sister probably would have let that drunk drive home just to make sure she didn't tick off a big tipper. Kelly has been one step away from getting fired ever since she walked in the door of the casino. She's always bending the rules way too close to breaking them. She sails in late, sneaks out early, plays the slots on the way to or from the john even though she's technically still on duty. You're a helluva lot more mature than she will ever be. How old are you, anyhow?"

"Sixteen."

"Holy shit! Not only did you risk getting the casino shut down by the State Liquor Board, you could have gotten me busted for statutory rape if we had done more than politely say good-night after going to Buddy's Burger Barn."

"I didn't mean for anything bad to happen. Kelly made it sound so simple, so harmless. When I met you, it was the very best thing that had ever happened to me in my whole entire life. I just wanted the night to last forever—or at the very least for it to last long enough to be okay for you to love me."

I waited for Hugh to slam the door on his way out, never look back. Instead, he asked if I'd mind taking a walk, so he could talk to Mom.

When I came back, Mom said Hugh was going to start coming to church with us on Sundays, and to dinner afterwards. Even though it would be almost a year before my seventeenth birthday, she not only gave me permission to date guys my age . . . she actually encouraged me to start dating! If it wasn't on a school night, if I made sure I was home by curfew, not one minute late. If I promised to call her or Kelly for a ride if my date started drinking, or I wound up at a party where the other kids were using drugs.

"I want you to get to know young men much closer to your own age. After you turn seventeen, I'll sign the consent form if you and Hugh still want to get married."

I was so stunned that I couldn't even speak. Hugh must have told Mom his intentions were honorable, and he must have said he loved me and wanted to marry me! How in the world would I survive all those months of going through the motions of dating other guys?

Hugh's eyes insisted that even without the heavy makeup and

Kelly's magic bra, I was still the woman of his dreams. It didn't matter that I was only sixteen. It didn't matter that we'd have to wait a while to make all our wonderful dreams come true.

It didn't take long for the word to get out that the town's strictest mother was suddenly allowing her daughter to date. I got invited out almost every Saturday night, made sure I paid my own way, and carefully explained that somebody already had my heart and soul.

Hugh and I got married on St. Patrick's Day the year I turned seventeen. I carried a bouquet with shamrocks and white lilies.

I was thrilled when the drugstore test confirmed I was pregnant in August. Hugh was petrified. As much as he loved children, I could tell he was terrified that he might lose me and our child—just like he'd lost Raven and her baby.

When I went into premature labor the night before St. Patrick's Day, it was almost like history repeating itself. I was in my eighth month just like Raven. Just like Raven, it felt like something was going terribly wrong.

The doctor didn't seem to be the least bit worried after she examined me.

"Twins often decide to come a little early. Dad, do you want to scrub up and join us in the delivery room?"

Poor Hugh looked pale as a ghost and none too steady on his feet, but he was right there—holding my hand every minute of every hour until Connor and Dillon doubled the size of our family.

We obviously didn't have Grandma's corned beef and cabbage that year, but having our special dinner on St. Patrick's Day to celebrate the luck of the Irish has been an honored Murtagh family tradition ever since.

I filled Grandma's biggest pot a little early this year, got Hugh to help me put the corned beef, cabbage, potatoes, and carrots in the refrigerator so somebody else could warm them up just in case Emily and Anne decide to follow in their big brothers' footsteps, and arrive early!

THE END

# ONE KISS BETWEEN STRANGERS
## Led To A Lifetime Of Happiness

Outside the window of my gift and candle shop, I noticed a dark-haired man slip into the alcove and then peek out as if watching for someone down the street . . . as if someone were following him.

He opened the door to my shop and stepped inside, jingling my shamrock wind-chime. Hoping he wasn't dangerous, I frowned. He responded with a forced smile.

"Hello. Are you looking for a St. Patrick's Day gift?" I asked, pretending he wasn't acting weird. I hoped this wouldn't take long. I wanted to close in a few minutes and head to my friend's St. Patrick's Day party.

The man came a few steps closer, and in the bright track lighting, I noticed his kind green eyes and attractive features. His brows were thick and dark, like his hair and he had a slight five-o'clock shadow.

"Actually, I'm hiding from—"

The door opened again, and before I had time to see who was entering, the man pulled me close and kissed my lips—a quick, firm, intriguing kiss. Just as abruptly, he stepped back, releasing me.

What on earth? I'm sure my mouth dropped open. I was too stunned to speak. What was going on here? I searched his tension-filled face for the answer.

"Quinn, what are you doing kissing her?" The woman who'd entered demanded in a shrill tone.

I held my breath. Dear Lord, please don't let her be his wife.

"Denise. What a surprise to see you, here." He motioned toward me and glanced down at my nametag. "This is my new girlfriend, Jill."

His words, combined with his Irish accent, jumbled my thoughts.

Girlfriend? What in blazes is he talking about?

He turned his head and winked at me, so the woman couldn't see. "Jill, meet Denise." He indicated the dark-haired vixen, with bright red lips and thick eyeliner.

Denise glared at me. I didn't know whether to play along or call the police.

"Nice to meet you."

I offered my hand, but Denise snarled her lip as if she might bite me.

"Quinn! How could you? We're dating!"

"No," he said in a gentle voice. "We only went out twice, and then, decided to see other people, remember?"

10

"But I don't want to see other people." Tears welled in her eyes and her voice lowered to a whimper. "I want to see only you. How long have you been going out with her?"

"A couple weeks."

Denise's cherry red mouth grew tighter, and a tear trailed black mascara down her cheek. "I don't believe you. I don't think she even knows you." She scowled at me. "What's his last name?"

"She knows my last name is O'Brien," Quinn said.

"Be quiet," she snapped at him, then speared me with her sharp blue gaze. "What's his middle name?"

"I . . . um, don't believe we exchanged that information, yet," I murmured.

What had I gotten myself into? I did not want to be a part of him breaking up with her. Obviously, she loved him, and he didn't return her feelings.

Denise stabbed a lethal red fingernail toward him.

"See, I knew you weren't dating her."

"Why would I kiss her if I wasn't dating her?"

"That was a fake kiss, just a peck. Not like the one you gave me on our last date."

"Listen, Denise, I'm sorry; it's over," Quinn said in a calm tone, but with an edge of finality. "You will find the right man for you, one day. Now, if you'll excuse us." He stepped closer to me. "We have a date."

Denise headed toward the exit, glancing back once, and slammed the door on her way out.

Quinn went to the window and peered out.

"I bet she'll wait out there for me."

"What's going on?" I asked, hands on my hips, determined to get to the bottom of this strange situation he'd dragged me into.

"She's stalking me, sort of. She isn't dangerous or anything, but she's driving me crazy. We only went out twice, and she thinks that means a committed relationship. She called me a dozen times a day, at the office, everywhere." He moved toward me. "I'm sorry I kissed you—well, not really because it was a nice kiss—but I should've asked your permission, first." He smiled, and unbelievably, I found him even more appealing than before.

A wave of heat washed over my face. Yes, it had been a nice kiss. A latent thrill spun through me.

Hold on a minute, Jill. He's just broken up with his girlfriend. He's probably a heartbreaker, a real-life Casanova, I thought.

"It was a spur of the moment thing, the kiss," he said. "I read your shirt—Kiss Me I'm Irish—then checked your finger to make sure you weren't wearing a wedding band. I made a snap decision, hoping if

Denise thought I was dating someone else, she wouldn't bother me, anymore."

"Ah."

Everything made perfect sense, now.

"Do you have a boyfriend who's going to kill me?"

He peered into the back room.

I shook my head, not wanting to remember my last boyfriend—a total loser who borrowed my car all the time, ran up my phone bill, and ate all my food.

"You're safe."

"So, you're Jill?"

Quinn offered his hand, and I shook it.

"Yes. I have a feeling you really are Irish, straight from the old sod."

"Aye. You have the right of it, lass," he said in a pronounced, lilting accent.

How adorable. I'd always loved a true Irish accent, and coming from such sensual lips, it was almost entrancing.

Uncomfortable with my growing attraction to him, I strode behind the checkout counter. "Would you be interested in a candle or perhaps some green bath salts?" I said, because I couldn't think of anything else to say.

"Will they turn the water green?"

"Yes."

"Hmm." He leaned on the counter.

"I've seen a river turned green, and I drank my fair share of green beer, but I swear I've never had a green bath. I'll take a half dozen."

"You're kidding."

"Nope."

He dug out his wallet.

I laughed and picked up six one-pound bags of the bath salts.

"Oh, and a couple of candles for my sister." He placed a green one and a white one on the counter. "Do you make these?"

"Sure do." I shot him a look from the corner of my eye. "I know a charity purchase when I get one."

"I'm owing you a debt of gratitude for rescuing me from Denise. That woman would worry the warts off a toad!"

Though I still felt bad for Denise, I chuckled at his comment.

"Do you have a back door I could escape through?"

"Yes, but it leads out onto the same street."

I handed him the change and bagged his purchase.

With a curse, he paced back and forth.

"When will you be closing?"

"Seven."

He looked at his watch. "Fifteen minutes." He grinned, his eyes

12

twinkling with mischief. "A lovely lass such as yourself, Jill, surely has a date tonight."

"Nope."

He crossed himself, glanced toward the heavens, and mouthed thank you.

I snorted to cover how incredibly flattered I felt.

"I'd like it if you would have a drink with me."

I had learned long ago if something seemed too good to be true, it probably was.

"So Denise will leave you alone?"

"Well, that would be one reason. The other would be—I'd like to get to know you better."

"Oh really?"

I asked, skeptically.

"It's O'Brien, and yes."

I grinned.

"All right." One drink. What harm could there be in that?

While I started my closing routine, he kept a watch out the window.

"I don't believe it. She's still out there. What a harpy she is. I'll never go on a blind date, again."

I glanced up from closing out the register.

"Why would you go on a blind date?"

I asked, trying not to stress the word you. He was gorgeous enough to get his own dates, unless he had hidden flaws.

"Favor to a coworker."

When we left the shop, Denise was standing in the shadows of a doorway across the street. I felt sorry for her. But I was also concerned she might not be as harmless as she appeared. What if she took out her pain and anger on me for "stealing" Quinn away from her? A cool breeze penetrated my jacket, and I shivered.

Glancing back, I didn't see her following us. Soon, I forgot about her and concentrated on the hunky Irishman beside me. As he talked, his lilting but faint accent charmed me, and made me want to smile.

The streets were not as crowded as they'd been earlier, but the pub we had our hearts set on was overflowing. Standing room only inside. An elderly couple approached, and Quinn opened the door for them.

"I'm not brave enough to jump into that mosh pit."

He let the door close back, shutting off the noise from inside.

"I was invited to a St. Patrick's Day party. Why don't you come with me?"

"You mean it?"

He sent me a boyish grin. The lights from the pub lit up half his face and defined his square jaw.

"Yes. It'll be fun."

The thought of getting to know him around a group of friends and acquaintances felt more comfortable than being alone. He seemed like a good guy, but who knew?

We continued down the street. I glanced at the six-pound bag of bath salts and candles he was lugging around.

"I bet you're tired of carrying all those."

"Do I look that weak?"

"No."

From the corner of my eye, I glanced at his strong-looking broad shoulders and wondered what he would look like without his shirt. One thing was certain, those jeans showed off his buns to perfection.

"That's my Jeep at the corner," he said. "Where is the party?"

I hadn't driven to work that day because I knew I wouldn't be able to get my car into and out of the blocked streets. I'd taken the bus. Now, I either had to ride with a man I barely knew, or walk seven blocks.

Turns out, I had worried for no reason, although I remained on guard. We arrived late to Laura's house, and the party was in full swing.

"This is Quinn," I said, as we entered and motioned to the smiling man behind me. The warmth of the big house combined with the luscious scents of smoked salmon, Irish stew, and walnut mince tarts made me feel welcome, and hungry.

"Quinn." Laura's mouth dropped open. "You two are dating?"

"Um."

I glanced at Quinn who had gone slightly pale.

"Yeah," he said.

"I see." Laura frowned.

"What's wrong?" I asked.

"I'll tell you, later."

Laura gave me a final glare and stalked away.

"What is going on?"

"Denise is Laura's boyfriend's sister," Quinn whispered. "We went on a double date with them. He's the one who set us up."

"Oh."

Yikes. This couldn't be good. What if Denise showed up here?

Deciding to put my worrying on the back burner for now, I had a green beer and potato scones with Quinn. Afterward, we danced to the live Irish music and drank shamrock cocktails.

"Ah, this reminds me of home," he said close to my ear as we danced to a ballad called "Mary of Tralee."

His warm breath on my skin sent a shiver down my arms.

"Do you miss Ireland?"

"Aye," he said as if the word were a normal part of modern-day

14

language. His tone was wistful and his gaze far away.

I wanted to hug him, comfort him if he was feeling homesick.

"How long have you been in the U.S.?"

"Five years. I lived in Boston a couple years before moving here."

Out of the corner of my eye, I noticed someone with long dark hair standing in a doorway watching us, it was Denise. Her eyes were red, and her mascara was smeared.

"Denise has arrived," I said, for Quinn's ears only.

He stiffened.

"Oh, dear God."

"She's been crying."

"Dammit. I shouldn't be here. I don't want to hurt her, anymore. Do you want to go?"

"That would probably be best."

The song ended, and we left the dance floor as the band struck up a livelier tune. We would have to walk right past Denise to exit the room.

Before we reached her, she ran, crying, down the hallway.

John and Laura glared at us as we approached.

"I'm so sorry," Quinn said. "I never meant to hurt her. We only went out twice. It just wasn't going to work out."

"I'm sorry, too. I'll call you, tomorrow," I told Laura.

I felt like a traitor, making Laura angry this way, but I also sympathized with Quinn. If he wanted to stop dating Denise, he had every right. Besides, I was starting to really like him.

Outside, the fresh cold air chilled the sweat on my skin. I'd forgotten how much exercise dancing could be.

Quinn escorted me to his Jeep, and I gave him directions to my house.

We were quiet while riding. I was thinking of poor Denise. How could someone fall so desperately in love after only two dates? I glanced at Quinn's masculine profile, and his hand slung casually over the steering wheel. Well, maybe it wasn't so hard to see how Denise would be drawn to him. He was the type who grew on you after a few smiles and teasing remarks.

At my building, I led the way up to my second-floor apartment.

"I want to see you, again," Quinn said, in a slightly raspy voice, his eyes a shade darker in the night.

"Are you sure?"

"Of course. Will you go out on a real date with me next Friday night?"

"Yes, I will." I smiled.

"Again, I'm sorry about the kiss in your shop, but . . . I find I'm craving another one, now."

15

My jacket was suddenly too hot, despite the icy air.

"Then, you aren't sorry?" I teased.

With a quirk of his lips, he shook his head.

"I enjoyed it, but it was too brief."

I slid my fingers into his dark hair and met his lips with my own. After a second of tentative exploration, we delved into a kiss, such as I have never before experienced. If sex could be captured in a kiss, this would've been it. He gathered me to him, and we indulged in another long moment of passion.

He groaned deep in his throat, released me, and moved back. Breathing hard, I held onto the doorjamb as his dark gaze moved from my eyes to my lips. He appeared a bit hypnotized, and I felt the same way.

"That was some Irish kiss." His accent grew heavier, making me wish I knew him better so I could invite him in.

"Yeah." I jiggled the key in the lock, and it finally turned. "Thank you for the wonderful evening."

"Thank you as well. I'll call you."

"Okay. Goodnight."

I went in and closed the door behind me. Wow! What a kiss. What a man!

"Jill, I can't believe you're going out with Quinn. He dumped Denise," Laura said on the phone the next day.

"It was two dates, one of which was a blind date. What's the big deal?" I asked.

"She's hurt, and she's John's sister. That's the big deal."

"Quinn didn't want to go out with her, anymore. Now, she's stalking him."

"She has a bit of a clinging issue, but that doesn't make it hurt any less. She has a major crush on him."

A wave of guilt washed over me because I was developing a crush on him, too.

"I understand, but she needs to move on," I said, gently. "She'll get over him in time."

"Jill, please, I'm asking you as a friend to not see him, anymore."

A fuse of anger lit inside me. Laura and I were friends, but not best friends. Sometimes, we didn't talk for weeks.

"How can you ask that of me?"

"Because John is angry, and since you're my friend, he's blaming me. He thinks I introduced you two."

"Well, you didn't. And John is the one with the problem. Sorry, but I like Quinn a lot, and we're going out on Friday."

After a few more words, I hung up the phone. If Laura were a true friend, she wouldn't try and prevent me from seeing a man I liked.

16

Quinn and I went out on Friday and several times over the next month. The more I got to know him, the more he charmed me . . . the more I wanted to listen to his lilting accent and gaze into his green eyes, forever. Hard to believe, but our kisses kept getting hotter. Quinn and I both wanted them to lead to something else, but we always restrained ourselves.

Sometimes, during the day or in the evenings, I felt as if someone were watching me. Even when Quinn and I went on dates, I sensed someone might be following us, but I never saw anyone. I had never been paranoid before I'd met Denise, and I hoped her anxiety wasn't rubbing off on me.

On the one-month anniversary of our first meeting, Quinn invited me to his house for dinner and a movie. He made me stay in the Jeep for five minutes while he made final preparations. What was he up to? I shivered with excitement.

When he took me inside, I was surprised to see candles lit throughout the house—many of which he'd bought at my shop. The scents of shamrock, fresh grass and flowers from the candles reminded me spring was almost here. And the scent of food made my stomach growl. He led me to the dining room and seated me at a candlelit table. Soft Celtic music played in the background. He served Shepherd's Pie and set a frosty mug of Irish beer by my plate.

"Thank you. This is lovely."

After we talked and laughed over dinner, he escorted me onto his private deck where a whirlpool large enough for two frothed and bubbled with green water. The scent was familiar.

"You used the bath salts?"

"Aye, my lady."

"Won't the salt ruin your pipes?"

"No, it's a pipe-less whirlpool."

"When you asked me to bring a swimsuit, I thought we were going swimming."

"You can call this swimming if you want, just in a tiny, hot, green pool."

I laughed and went back inside to change into my swimsuit.

Ten minutes later, we sank into the heavenly hot water. The jets massaged and tickled my back and legs. I watched Quinn through the steam. Part of his chest rose above the water, and it was indeed a mouth-watering chest with muscles that reminded me of an Olympic swimmer.

He relaxed back, smiling at me, and I had the urge to kiss him. I moved across the tub and straddled his lap. He tugged me to him and delivered a kiss even steamier than the water. Under the water, he slipped his fingers over my skin and inched them beneath my bikini top. He toyed with my nipples, and arousal rushed through me.

Moaning, I clung to his neck as he deepened the kiss.

Something fell onto the deck with a thump, startling me. Glancing toward the sound, I thought one of his candles had toppled over. But the flame looked more like a sparkler. Quinn pulled me from the tub, rushed me inside the house, and slammed the door.

What sounded like rapid gunfire, followed.

I screamed and dropped to the floor. After a few seconds, all was silent again.

"What the hell was that?"

"Firecrackers." Quinn cursed and yanked the door open. He sprinted across his lawn and through his fence gate.

"Firecrackers?" I muttered, slowly rising on trembling legs and peered out.

Who would throw firecrackers onto his deck? Surely, not Denise.

After yanking on my large T-shirt cover-up, I crept outside and saw that indeed, the debris lying on the deck was from a whole pack of firecrackers that had exploded in rapid succession.

A scream erupted beyond the gate.

"That's it, dammit! I'm getting a restraining order!" Quinn exclaimed, dragging a hysterical Denise through the gate.

She called him all sorts of vile names, and when she saw me, she threw a few curses my way.

An hour later, after the police had left—along with John and Laura, Quinn, and I, sat on his sofa. I was still stunned that Denise wanted to scare us so badly. She could actually hurt us next time.

My stomach ached. "It really makes me mad that she ruined our special evening," I said.

"I'm sorry you had to go through that." Though he sat two feet away from me, Quinn ran his fingers through my hair. "I suppose I never should've dragged you into this mess."

"How can you say that? If you hadn't come into my shop to hide from Denise, we never would've met."

He nodded.

"That's true."

I slid toward him on the sofa.

"I'm glad we met."

"You are?"

"Yes. More than glad. Thrilled and overjoyed."

I kissed him gently on the lips.

"So am I. I was just worried you would regret getting involved— especially after what happened, tonight."

"No."

We indulged in slow, open-mouthed kisses that seduced my senses and aroused my whole body.

18

He tugged aside the large T-shirt I wore over my bikini and stroked my back, my stomach, and my breasts. His fiery kisses combined with his delightful touch made me want to rip his clothes off.

"I want you, Quinn," I whispered against his mouth. "I want you, right now."

He groaned, his green eyes growing dark.

"Not as much as I want you." He took off my bikini, then stood and removed his clothes. He knelt before me at the sofa, and within moments after he put on a condom, we were making love. Magical shivers raced through me each time he moved. He gazed into my eyes while we shared that incredible experience, and I knew I would be thrilled to look into his green eyes, forever. I was thankful for our bizarre meeting, and knew it had been the luckiest day of my life.

Denise moved to Texas and a few months later, Laura told me she'd married a cowboy. A year after Quinn and I had met, on St. Patrick's Day, we got married in Ireland, in the traditional way and in the midst of his large, extended family. They welcomed me with open arms, and laughed at our meeting story that began with a kiss between strangers.

THE END

# UNDERCOVER IRISH
## Why I Couldn't Let Anyone
## Know My True Heritage

I stood in a packed bar, singing in merriment, one of the many Irish pub songs. It was Saint Patrick's Day, and as was tradition, I went with friends to a bar (as there were no pubs in my town), and drank. The green beers flowed, the shamrock shots were slammed against the counter as drunken person after drunker person downed them like it was the last source of refreshment they would ever receive. The smell of alcohol and sweat permeated the small bar. It was sweltering, but everyone was drunk, so they didn't seem to notice.

Personally, I hated Saint Patrick's Day; it was only a reminder of the lie I was living and the double life I was leading. I sipped on a Guinness all night. I was smart enough not to get drunk, so I kept my drinking down to one beer. I stood there in my black pants, revealing green shirt, and a silly "Kiss me, I'm Irish" sticker on the lapel of my overcoat. My friend, Kelly, made me wear it. Pretending to be happy, I butchered the pub song, "Hurry Up, Harry," along with the rest of the crowd. I was deep in song, when a sense of foreboding came over me.

I looked up. From across the crowded space, I could see three people enter the bar: a petite redhead with curly hair accompanied by two very large men. I recognized them all. I decided to run into the restroom to calm myself and hope none of the newcomers spotted me. I had been living in town for seven years: working, having friends, and going out; now, it would all come to an end. I didn't want to go back to the old days when I couldn't get a job, and I was constantly teased. I refused to let that happen. Slowly, I manipulated my way through the crowd, partially slipping on the beer stained floor several times, before finally reaching the overly occupied restroom.

I knew I could not hide in the bathroom all night. My friends might worry. As flaky as they sometimes were, I knew they would not leave the bar without me. Frantically, I paced the small confines of the restroom, coming up with a plan. I could wait until someone came in the restroom after me, claim to be sick, and hopefully slip past the three new patrons in the bar and get home before being spotted. Feeling at ease with my plan, I waited for someone to come after me.

Thirty minutes later, when no one came in the bathroom, I panicked. I leaned over the porcelain sink—careful not to touch the filthy edges, and looked into the mirror. Finally, I liked the reflection I saw. With the help of four-inch heels, I stood at five-feet seven. My skin was flawless, I sported a light golden tan, my blue eyes shimmered, and my straight blonde hair cascaded down my back. Though sometimes, I talked slower than everyone else, my English was perfect. Suddenly, like a light bulb going off in my head, the answer came. No one would recognize me. At least, I hoped not. I was sure that two out of the three wouldn't, anyway. I looked completely different. Feeling full of confidence about my new look, I stepped out of the restroom and smacked into the one person I was hoping to avoid.

I briefly looked up at him, which was my first mistake. Even after all those years, he affected me. I felt a spark of energy and I took a moment to remember the past. He had grown since I last saw him, and he was more handsome than I remembered. He was at least six-one, completely towering over me. His short dark hair was combed back with a few strands resting on his forehead. I stared into his smoky gray bedroom eyes, covered by his long, sexy eyelashes, and I tried not to jump into his arms. His creamy vanilla skin begged to be licked. His face was perfectly angular; I wanted to stroke my fingers along his jaw line to feel his smooth masculine edges. It seemed I had been staring at him for ages, remembering him, memorizing his beauty; but in actuality it was only a second. I quickly recovered from my trance, mumbled my apologies for bumping into him, and scurried away.

I battled my way through the masses, arrived at the bar, and ordered a shamrock shot. My heart felt like it was going to beat through my chest.

"All right, you finally decided to do more than sip on that beer." I heard my friend, Kelly, cheer me on as I guzzled my shot in one gulp. She patted me on the back, "Hey we're all Irish, today. Get drunk!"

Thank God, I knew my limits and the Shamrock shooter would not send me teetering over the edge, but hopefully it would calm me down.

"Did you see those gorgeous men walk in about half an hour ago?" She pointed to them. "There they are!"

Angie piped in.

"Oh my gosh, did I ever. I could definitely handle Seamus and Magus over there."

Kelly looked at her.

"Seamus? Where did you get that from?"

"You know those trashy Irish romances. I have always wanted to get with an Irishman. I heard them talking; they all have Irish accents."

Kelly's interest in them, suddenly seemed to get greater.

"Hmmm, just off the boat Irishmen, ay. Now, that is tempting!"

I internally rolled my eyes at both of them as they continued their conversations of what they would like to do with the two Irishmen, as long as they didn't talk. It seems neither one of them thought the Irish accent was sexy. Out of the corner of my eye, I saw "him" approach the bar. I leaned on the bar for support.

"Don't I know yis?" His bulging arms were resting on the bar counter, and he looked me directly in the eye.

"Uh, I don't think so." I pushed myself away from the bar, he grabbed my arm and said, "I think yis know me." He smiled then, displaying perfectly straight white teeth. "Alister," he put his hand out. I accepted. "Patricia, nice to meet you, Alister. I must get going, now."

I yanked my arm free and trotted away. Kelly came running after me. "Tricia wait up." I stopped. "What's wrong with you. The sexy Seamus wants you. His accent is thick, but you don't need him to say anything." She winked. I gave her an incredulous look. "Okay, okay, what's really wrong?"

"Nothing, I just need to go home, I think the Shamrock made me sick. I'm going to catch a cab and go home."

"You sure?"

I saw the concern in Kelly's eyes.

"Yes, go back in, and have fun. Remember everyone is Irish today, so drink until you can't remember your name. Then, take a cab and go home."

I heard her mumble under her breath, "Hopefully with someone."

I hopped in a cab, went home, and hoped I would not run into Alister McFadden, again.

No such luck. The next week, my boss called me into his office.

"Patricia, we found a replacement for Rob. We got you a new partner. He is a transfer from our Dublin office—"

Please God, no; Please God, no. I chanted a silent prayer, hoping it was just a dumb coincidence. My boss's next five words shattered that theory.

"His name is Alister McFadden…" The boss kept talking, but soon after he said Alister McFadden, my mind reeled, and I heard nothing. At that moment, I felt like the unluckiest person in the world. "So you leave in two weeks." I was so caught up in my own musings, that I had no idea where I was going in two weeks.

"Where am I going?" I blurted. I was too thrown off to worry about appearances. My boss gave me an exasperated look and answered "Chicago!"

You and Alister will be taking over the Midwest region and giving the West Coast to Bobby and his team."

If it were physically possible, my jaw would have hit the floor. I recuperated as best I could and left his office. It was days like that, that made me wish I still went to church. Because that is how I would have spent my lunch break: in a confessional, asking for forgiveness—hoping that would make Alister go away. Instead, I spent lunchtime in the park.

I sat on the bench, and for a moment, wondered what would happen if Alister did not reveal my cover. I could continue working at a job I loved. I would have friends, a great social circle, but I would still be lonely. I couldn't have a lover, a boyfriend, and definitely not a husband. It didn't matter; I had done fine without one most of my life. I had my health, my family, and the life I always imagined. I was the pretty girl, free from ridicule, desired by many, taken by none. I knew I couldn't live a lie for the rest of my life, I just needed a few more years; and then, I would change towns and be myself. By then, I would have built up an excellent sales history. I could get any job I wanted. I just wished I had more time—which I didn't since Alister was going to be my sales partner. I sat on the bench and looked at a patch of clovers. How ironic, I thought. I walked over, knelt in front of them, and discovered a four-leaf clover. I picked it up. I sat back on the bench twirling it between my thumb and middle finger.

"Supposed to bring you luck," I heard Alister comment behind me. I didn't look up. He took the unoccupied seat next to me on the bench and continued. "Do you know what the four-leaf clover means?"

"Yes, it's a rare genetic anomaly."

"Now Patty, I know you don't believe that. An Irish girl like you." He pulled the clover from my hands and pointed to the leaves. "This one represents hope," He pointed to the next one. "This one represents faith." I was looking down at the clover. He moved his index finger under my chin and gently lifted it until our eyes met, and he persisted. "This one . . ." his fingers stroked the petal as his eyes bore into mine, "represents love…" There was a lingering moment where it felt like time stood still, and the air around us crackled. I was the first to glance away. I glimpsed in his direction, and he was beaming at me. He looked down at the last leaf. "And this one is for luck. Luck of the Irish. How appropriate that you would pick it."

"Yeah, lucky indeed," I murmured under my breath. Not feeling lucky at all.

Alister leaned back against the bench, crossed his right ankle so it was resting on his left thigh, and laid his right arm on the top of the bench behind me. The gesture of crossing his leg caused his thigh to brush against mine. My heart beat a little faster; and I wished Alister didn't affect me as much. Since I was a little girl, I had a crush on him. Sitting next to him in that moment, I realized it never went away.

"So I see yuh changed, Patty." He scrutinized my entire body. I felt like an animal on display. He leaned to whisper in my ear. "You look nice; but personally, I prefer freckles, green eyes, and fire red hair on a nice Irish girl." He stood then. "If you find her, let me know."

Then, he walked away. Tears clouded my eyes as I watched him leave.

That evening, while doing my nightly rituals, I thought about what Alister said. I took my contacts out, and stared at my green-eyed reflection in the mirror. My face was still golden as I had just had my spray-on treatment two days prior. But I knew I should have been looking at milky white skin accentuated with freckles, brought out by curly, fire red hair. I was a true Irish girl no matter how much I tried to hide it. I stood in the mirror reflecting on how I got to that point in my life.

I was born in Sligo, Ireland. I moved to the United States when I was fourteen. I attended a small Catholic school; where they held me back a year because of my accent. Even though I spoke English, they said, no one could understand me. I went from being a straight-A student, to being held back. I was taunted endlessly by classmates. "Freckle Face," "Leprechaun," "Shamrock Devil," "Potato-eating filthy Irish girl,", were some of the lighter insults I got. I grew to hate the town and hate everyone around. Every time I looked in the mirror, I saw what they saw. My life was a living hell. I had thought about killing myself and ending it all. I had no friends, never had a boyfriend, and everyone refused to eat at my table during lunch. I had thought things would get better when I went to high school, I was wrong.

My graduation present was a trip back home for the summer. It felt good to be myself and liked for it. I spent my summer with my childhood crush: Alister. When I returned back to the States to go to college, things didn't get better. Maybe if I had gone to school somewhere like Chicago or New York, life would have been better. But my town had very few Irish people; in fact, our family was the only one. I didn't have the grades for a scholarship, and my hardworking, middle-class parents could not afford to send me out of state. I continued to stare at my reflection in the mirror, and with a mental shrug, I left the bathroom and went to bed. As I laid on my soft silk sheets, I was determined not to let Alister affect me or ruin the life I made for myself.

We left for Chicago two weeks later as planned. Because the company planner booked the flight, I sat next to Alister. I tried to ignore him. I opened a book and began to read, pretending the smell of his sandalwood cologne didn't have my heart beating faster. I felt him staring at me, but I continued to ignore his overwhelming presence as best I could.

"Lovely American accent you have, matches your blue eyes and golden tanned skin."

Alastar leaned over and whispered in my ear. Though he was being sarcastic, the feathered caress of his breath as he uttered the words sent tiny shivers down my spine. I remained calm, turned my head to face him and replied.

"Nice accent, I noticed you don't talk like the people in Sligo."

My face was upturned, and I gave him the meanest look I could muster.

He simply nodded and smiled, "Touché."

Though to many, he had a strong Irish accent; to me, it barely existed. He had definitely worked on lessening it—which was understandable. He dealt with many clients from all over the world; and they needed to be able to understand him. However, it didn't matter I had one piece of ammo to throw against him, and I was intent on using it. I continued in my tirade.

"Are the pots calling the kettles black?"

"Why?"

It was a simple question. I almost feigned ignorance—if it wasn't for the sincerity in his smoke gray eyes. He looked hurt. And it hurt me knowing I put it there.

"You don't know what it was like, Alister. Growing up the only Irish in town wasn't easy. I spent every moment here, alone. I did what I had to do to fit in. I know it seems like a cop-out, but I was tired of being isolated and ostracized."

I was almost pleading with him to understand. I didn't want his contempt. I know that by changing, I was spitting on our Irish heritage, denying myself, and denying him.

He did what I least expected him to do. He folded me in his arms and held me. There on the plane, leaning over the armrest, he gave me what I yearned for since moving to America: acceptance. I didn't want to leave the security of his embrace, but he pulled back. I tried to turn my face to quickly wipe away the tears trapped in my eyes that threatened to fall. He grabbed my face before I could. He very tenderly took his index fingers and wiped them away. Then, he bent his head down and placed a gentle kiss in the middle of my forehead. The softness of his lips did little to ease me. I only desired more of him. Too soon, our intimate encounter ended, and he leaned back in his seat. Starring at nothing in particular, especially me, he informed me, "I think you will like Chicago. It's a lot different than Utah."

He leaned his seat back, folded his arms over his chest, and went to sleep.

He was right. Chicago was a lot different than Utah. I had never seen such an assorted mix of people. From the moment I got off the plane at O'Hare International Airport—which incidentally, was named after an Irish-American—I noticed the diversity. People were tanned, mocha, caramel, ivory, ecru, and porcelain white, among many other shades. Alister had to nudge me to keep me walking toward baggage claim and not stopping to people watch.

"You ready for this?" We were standing in baggage claim watching for our bags to appear on the carousel. Correction, he was inspecting for the luggage, I was observing all the people around me. I craned my neck to look him in the eye. "Ready for what?"

"The mayor is Irish," he said with pride.

It was then that I felt like a fool. I went from one rural town to another. I'd moved from Sligo to a small town in Utah. I never even ventured to Salt Lake City. I was sheltered, and I let my lack of knowledge change me. I hated who I was, and I hated who I had been. Alister and I would be in Chicago for a while; I planned on taking in the city and making some changes to myself.

"Wow, you look different!" Alister blurted when I came down to the lobby of the hotel to meet him.

Over a week had passed since my last spray tan application. My Irish skin was more apparent. I was no longer covered from head to toe in business attire—which was what he usually saw me wearing. I was dressed to go out. My arms were exposed, and my cleavage—though small—was on display. I wasn't wearing my contacts. Though my hair was still straight and blonde, I felt freer than I had in a long time.

"Uh well, I—"

"You look gorgeous." He amended, "You have always looked gorgeous."

People lied and words could be false, but from the look of admiration and the changing of his eyes to charcoal, I knew he meant every word he said. Floored, I could only respond meekly. "Thank you." I glanced away and cleared my throat, trying to escape the trance that the desire in his eyes held. "So, uh, when, I mean where . . ." I stumbled over my words. "Where are we going?"

The brilliant and bright smile he bestowed upon me was priceless. "We're going dancing."

We ended up at the Gaelic Center. I had the time of my life. He took me ceili dancing. We laughed and danced down the line, face-to-face with other couples. It had been such a long time since I danced to music from my homeland; I had forgotten how much I loved to dance. When we arrived back at the hotel, he walked me to my room.

"I had a great time, Alister. Thank you!"

"It's my pleasure," he bowed down and kissed my hand, "my fair Irish Queen . . . Maeve."

He looked up at me and winked, and then, he departed to his adjoining room. Queen Maeve is what he called me while growing up. It was a childhood taunt. I don't know why my mother would give

26

me a middle name after the Celtic god of intoxication and the ancient mean warrior Queen Maeve that is buried in Sligo. Somehow, though, when Alister said it that time, it didn't seem mean or taunting. In fact, his voice had lowered several seductive octaves. The warrior Queen Maeve was also known for her sexual prowess. If the Maeve reference had that sexual innuendo, he was in for a big surprise.

The incessant knocking on the door jarred me awake. I checked the clock on the nightstand; the bright red letters displayed five-thirteen. It occurred to me to ignore the door, but the way the person was pounding, I thought surely at any moment, they would knock it down. I heard no alarm, nor commotion, so it couldn't have been a fire. I got up from the bed without any thought of putting on a robe, and I walked across the carpeted floor in my comfortable flannel socks, to the door. When I looked through the peephole, I was surprised to see it was Alister, completely dressed, with something behind his back. I opened the door, forgetting that I was only wearing a nightshirt and nothing else.

"Happy Birthday!" he pulled a bouquet of roses from behind his back.

"You were born at five-fourteen in the morning. I wanted to be the first to wish you a happy birthday. You're officially twenty-seven."

I took the proffered roses. They were beautiful—all twenty-seven of them. I gave him a drowsy smile.

"Thank you."

I moved out of the doorway to allow him entry. I walked over to the desk, and laid the roses on them. When I turned around, he was right behind me. He almost startled me. Feeling truly appreciative of the thought, I reached up on my tiptoes to give him a kiss on the cheek. He turned his face, and I ended up giving him a kiss on the mouth. Instead of chastising him, I decided to let it slide. After all, he had soft supple lips, and I had wanted to kiss him since he stepped into the small town Utah bar. Thinking to hell with it, it's my birthday, I leaned up again. This time, I purposefully aimed for his lips. He met me halfway, preparing for my thank you. His tongue invaded my mouth. I was thankful I had flossed, rinsed, and brushed my teeth before going to bed a few hours earlier. I knew he had done the same more recently. I could taste the mint in his mouth as my tongue massaged his. I don't know if it was the late time of night, the lack of sleep, or because it was Alister, but I didn't want him to leave—nor did I want us to stop. I wrapped my arms around his neck and leaned into him to enjoy our tongue duel. After a few minutes, Alister pulled away from the kiss, leaving my tongue mourning his absence, but did not stop completely. He grazed on the corner of my mouth, nibbled on my ear, and suckled on my neck; while his hands smoothed down the contours of my petite frame. My body was on fire. I was attuned to only him. I wanted to stop, I knew I should stop, but I couldn't

27

push him away. It was the silly dreams of childhood and fantasies of a teenager, but he was the only man I ever loved. I knew it had been almost ten years since I last saw him, although we kept in contact via email. We were grown, and I was holding onto childhood feelings. It was hard to let them go with his lips roaming my body as they were.

"I love you," he murmured. I know he didn't mean to let it slip because as soon as the words escaped his mouth, we both ceased movement. A pin could have dropped in the room and made a loud echo. We didn't speak, breathe, nor move. It was as if by keeping quiet, the words could be erased. Finally, he lifted his head to steady me.

"I didn't mean to let that slip."

I made a move to speak, but he put a finger over my lips to hush me. "But I meant it. Blonde, red, or green, I love you, Patty. I always have. You know that."

I didn't know what to say. I didn't even know if I believed him. How could I? I wanted to believe him. I did believe that he once loved me, but how could he love a sellout? That was exactly what I had become before he returned to my life. Though I internally questioned his love for me, it was then I knew without a doubt, I loved him. I loved him for who he was and who I was around him. He brought out the best in me, the Irish in me. But more importantly, he was the only one who knew me—the real me—and wanted me because of and in spite of who I was. I didn't know how to express my feelings and I didn't want to dispute his, so I poured all my emotions into my lips and transferred them to his.

What we shared was true passion. His hands searched the hem of my nightgown as our tongues danced the Irish dance of desire. When he found it, he raised it up over my head and off my body. From his sharp intake of breath, I could tell he was a bit startled to see me naked. The shimmering of his eyes and the shallowness of his breath let me know he liked what he saw. He took a moment to simply stare. He did a quick shake of the head, as if escaping some trance I held him under. He quickly removed his clothes and in two blinks of an eye, he stood naked before me.

He took his time to worship my body and sheathed himself before hovering over me. He gave me one last chance.

"Are you sure?" My tongue on his ear was my answer. Thankfully, we both spoke the same language: the language of desire. In one swift fluid motion, he penetrated the depths of my womanhood, breaking my barrier of innocence, causing me to scream in pain. He suspended his movements.

"I didn't know." He chanted. Tears clouded my eyes, partly from pain, partly from embarrassment. I didn't want him to stop. It felt right, but I knew I had just mortified him.

To my relief, he didn't continue. He just stayed there, cemented in his position, beads of sweat resting on his forehead from the effort of not moving and holding himself above my body. I felt the need to say something.

"When you spend your life lying about who you are on the outside it becomes impossible to let someone . . ." I gazed down at our joined bodies, "inside."

He regarded me, and in that moment, I truly knew he loved me. It was written plainly on his face. I swiped a tear out of the corner of his eye before his lips claimed mine in a soul-searching kiss. I kissed him back with all the love in my heart. There was no judgment, just understanding.

After several moments of reacquainting our mouths and tongues with each other, he continued his original pursuit. My body had adjusted to his. As he steered his ship in my ocean of pleasure, we rode the waves of passion together. I felt completely one with him. When completion came, he collapsed on top of me, before rolling over and pulling my body into the hollow of his arms. We both lay there in silence, trying to catch our breath.

"You know," he started, "I have been thinking." He rested his right arm behind his head while stroking my naked back with his left. "How did you convince people you weren't Irish with a name like O'Malley."

I tucked my head into his chest, ashamed of the answer. "I changed it to Smith." I peeked up at him, wanting to see his response, but his eyes and face were pointed toward the ceiling.

"You know you should get your name changed, again."

I let out a big sigh.

"Yes I know."

"I'm thinking, though," he continued, staring at the ceiling, "you shouldn't change it to O'Malley."

I crinkled my forehead in confusion. Finally, he looked down and stared me directly in my eye. "You should change it to McFadden." It took a moment before I grasped the gravity of what he was asking. As if to clarify, he got his naked body out of bed and knelt beside it on one knee. "Patricia Maeve O'Malley Smith, I have always loved you. You and only you. If you'll have me, I'm yours. Marry me."

What he didn't know was he already had me. Mind, body, and soul. I did change my name to a good, old-fashioned Irish one: Patricia O'Malley McFadden!

THE END

29

# MY IRISH COWBOY
## He Loved Me Despite My Klutziness, Superstitious Beliefs, And Fears

"Really, Donnie, I don't feel like going to the St. Patrick's Day party with you," I said to my older brother.

"Aw, come on! I want to have a few drinks, and I need a designated driver," he said. "My boss is picking up the tab for dinner and drinks. It'll be fun."

"Why can't you get one of the guys from work to bring you home?"

"Can't. They all either have a wife or girlfriend who'll be with them. And you know there aren't any taxis that come out here to the boondocks."

I sighed. I hadn't been out since Matt and I broke up six months ago. I had sworn off men for good. I even gave some thought to becoming a nun. Men were nothing but trouble, anyhow.

After Matt and I parted ways, Donnie moved into my house to help pay the rent.

"It'll do you good to go out," Donnie said. "Who knows? You might even learn to loosen up and have some fun. You used to look so nice, and now, you look sort of frumpy."

"What do you mean, frumpy? I still wear the same clothes and—"

"Well, your hair for one thing," he said. "You used to wear it down and kept it looking nice. Now, you tie it into a bun, and it makes you look old."

I caught a glimpse of myself in the hallway mirror and was shocked to realize that he was right. I had also gained a little weight, and my clothes were getting snug.

"Did I tell you that it's at Sean's home, and he'll be there, too? He and my boss have been friends for years. You do remember my college buddy, don't you?"

I raised my eyebrow. How could I ever forget Sean? He and my brother were four years older than me. The first time I met Sean, I was fifteen years old and had the biggest crush on him.

"I thought he got married?"

"Naw, he broke the engagement, and is still single. So, what do you say? Will you go with me, tonight?"

I looked at my brother who had been there for me when I was depressed over Matt. And when he realized that I needed help with the rent, he moved from his apartment to help me out.

"Okay, okay, so I'll go, but don't try fixing me up with any of those weirdos that you like to introduce me to."

Donnie laughed.

Although I was sure I would have a miserable time, I agreed to go. I did need to get out of the house. And it was a free meal.

I dressed in my black dress that fell just to the knees and low heels—just in case I did decide to dance. Besides, I knew the black dress showed off my red hair to my advantage. While I got the bright red hair and green eyes from our Irish father, Donnie got the blue eyes and blonde hair from our mother's German heritage.

The tavern was crowded, and we were led to the back room that Donnie's boss had rented for the night. An Irish band played folk music and sang. I sat between Donnie and one of his coworker's wives. Thankfully, Missy was friendly, and she spent time talking to me.

The band encouraged the audience to sing along with them. I recalled many of the songs from my grandparents, who used to play the Irish music at their home.

We were at the tavern about half an hour when a man came to our table and started talking to Donnie. I continued speaking with Missy. But then, Donnie introduced me to Melvin, someone he'd gone to high school with. Melvin had been in the other part of the tavern and noticed Donnie in the room.

"Hey, Lori, my friend wants to know if you'll dance with him," Donnie said. "It's okay, I know him from high school."

I looked at the short man with dark hair. There was something creepy about him.

"No thanks," I said, turning back to Missy.

"Oh, come on, Sis. One dance won't hurt you," he said.

I rolled my eyes and got up, going to the dance floor with the man.

"So, I don't remember you being Donnie's little sister," he said.

"That's because I wasn't in high school until you graduated," I said.

We took a few more dance steps, and out of nowhere, came three women who looked like gypsies. They headed straight for us, gibbering away in some language I didn't understand. One grabbed Melvin by his arm, while the other two grabbed both my arms.

"What the—"

They were followed by a bouncer for the tavern who snatched the women's hands off my arm. I stood in shock, not having any clue what was happening.

"You! All of you! Get out of here! This is a private party, and you can't be here," the bouncer said.

"Not until I keel her! She tryin' to take my man!"

31

"I don't even know your man," I said. I glanced around looking for Donnie, whom I was going to "keel" as soon as I found him.

"I'm sorry about this, Miss," the bouncer said.

"Not as sorry as my sorry ass brother will be when I find him. He insisted that I dance with this man!"

"What's going on?"

I looked up and saw Sean O'Brien—who put a protective arm around me.

"I'm afraid these gypsies invaded this party," the bouncer said.

Sean looked at the gypsy man who was leering at me and said, "Don't you ever come near this woman, again."

The three women started saying how I wanted to take their man, but another bouncer joined the first and they escorted the gypsies away.

"Are you okay, Lori?"

"I am now, thanks. But I'm so furious at Donnie. How could he tell me to dance with that man? I didn't even want to dance with him, and then, those women said they wanted to kill me."

Sean guided me back to the table. That's when Donnie appeared.

"So, what was all that ruckus about?" He asked.

I picked up my glass of water and threw it in his face.

"I'm so mad at you!"

He picked up a napkin and wiped his face.

"Why? What did I do?"

"You made me dance with that gypsy! His woman wanted to kill me, that's what! Right now, I just want to crawl under the table and make everyone quit staring at me," I hissed.

Donnie looked at me.

"Really? You mean I missed it all when I went to the men's room?"

I glared at him. Then, he turned to Sean.

"Good to see you, Sean. Do you remember my baby sister, Lori?"

Sean's eyebrows rose and he looked at me. "Yes, I recognized her out on the dance floor when the bouncer came in."

He gave me a smile.

I noticed his dimples and the way his green eyes met mine. I could've sworn I heard my grandmother saying, "Look into a man's eyes, and you'll look into his soul."

"You've grown up, Lori. I still remember you with your ponytail and freckles. And whatever happened to that dose of freckles I liked to tease you about?"

He tapped my nose with his finger.

A young woman came up behind my brother and grabbed his arm. "Hey, Susie!"

Donnie was dragged onto the dance floor by the woman he called

Susie. Just as well. Otherwise, I may have had my Irish dander get up again and throw something else at him.

Looking back into Sean's eyes, I felt myself blush. I hated blushing. It was annoying. So I tried to make the best of it.

"Yes, that's me: all grown up. So, how are you Sean?"

I thought he had to be one of the most handsome cowboys I'd ever laid eyes on. Sitting close to me, I could smell his soap. I was sure it was that Irish Spring stuff that my mom used to keep in the house. His reddish hair had darkened some, and that incredible smile could turn on a nun.

"Fine, fine. Thought I'd come home for a week or so to see my family."

"Where are you living, now? Last I heard, you were playing cowboy in Wyoming."

"Yes, I did play cowboy in the summers while in college; but now, I book the rodeos all over the country," he said. "I'm living in Colorado now. Can I get you something to drink?"

"I'm the designated driver, so a soda is what I'll have," I said.

Sean got up and Missy, sitting next to me, said, "My goodness. He's adorable. Is he really a cowboy?"

"Seems to be," I said, following his movement to the bar.

"Is he single?"

"Why, are you interested?"

"No, but if you aren't, my sister sure would be. I mean, the man exudes sex appeal."

"He sure does," I said. That, he did. Maybe I wasn't cut out for nun-hood after all, if I could still feel like this around a good-looking man.

"I heard people saying that those gypsy women wanted to kill you," Missy said. "Is that true?"

"Yes."

"I don't blame you for throwing that water in your brother's face. I'd have kicked him in the behind but good, if it were me."

"Here you go, Lori," Sean said, sitting down my drink and scooting his chair close to me. "It's loud in here, isn't it?"

About then, the band took a break, and we could finally hear one another. "So, tell me, Lori, what do you do for work since you graduated from college? You did graduate, didn't you?"

"Yes, I got my BA in nursing," I said, thinking that maybe I wouldn't mind him as a patient.

Just then, someone plugged the jukebox and "Mama, Don't Let Your Babies Grow Up To Be Cowboys" started to play. I looked at Sean, and he and I started laughing.

"Oh, boy! Yep, that's what my mama said often. 'Sean, be a doctor, be a lawyer, an engineer, anything but a cowboy.'"

"Do you regret not listening to her?"

"Not at all," he said, giving me a mischeivous grin. "If I remember right, your mama wanted you to become a nun. And I see that you didn't."

I laughed.

"Sometimes, I wonder if I should've."

"Oh, honey, I don't think so. To hide that gorgeous red hair and that body under an ugly black outfit, that would be a sin!" he said.

Once more, I felt the heat rising in my cheeks. I turned away and took a gulp of soda. Really, what was wrong with me? Men didn't generally affect me like this. The most provocative thoughts raced through my head. I envisioned him sitting atop a horse in his underwear and boots, smiling down at me. And boy, I'd enjoy taking him off that horse. I shook my head and decided it was time to focus on the music—the band was returning to the stage.

We laughed a lot that night. I found Sean to be quite the storyteller. I learned a lot about his life as a cowboy and how he learned about nursing.

When they finally played a song that we could dance to, I agreed to go out on the dance floor for the second time. There was a step down onto the floor, and as I took that step, I suddenly found myself on the floor.

"Whoa! I told you your drinks were too strong for you, didn't I?"

I looked up at Sean and saw the mischief in his eyes. But I didn't find it amusing when everyone stared at me—again. He leaned over and lifted me up. That's when I realized that the heel on my shoe had broken, and made me fall.

"Anyone have any glue with them?" Donnie asked, yelling into the crowd. "Little sister's shoe broke. Or better yet, is there a shoemaker in the house?"

That brought laughs to everyone, but me. I felt my face heating up, and I knew any minute I'd be red and blotchy.

Sean leaned over and whispered, "Are you okay?"

"I'm fine." I took my shoe off and headed back to the table.

"You aren't going to let a little thing like your shoe breaking keep you off the dance floor, are you?"

"I don't think I'm supposed to dance, tonight. I mean, with the first incident, now this one—maybe someone's trying to tell me something," I said.

He laughed at that.

"I do believe your little ole foot wouldn't fit into this big old cowpoke boot, or I'd take them off and give them to you."

I smiled.

"I guess you're right."

"Hey, just take off your shoes. We can dance fine like that."

I took them off, and headed to the dance floor once more. This time, they were teaching everyone an Irish folk dance.

"I've never been very good at this type of thing," I said to Sean.

He curtsied and said, "My lady, shall we learn to dance?"

So okay, I went left when everyone else went right. I stepped on Sean's toes every few steps, and I nearly tripped and fell on my face when we twirled. But I was having fun for a change.

By the end of the evening, I was sorry to see it end. But then, I had to find my brother whom I saw snuggled up to one of the girls from his office. He certainly seemed to have a good time flirting—and filling his gullet with green beer.

"Come on, Donnie, time to go home," I said. "Remember, I'm your designated driver."

"Oh, yeah, that's right. I'll see you later, Susie," he said.

We said goodnight to Sean and headed home.

I figured I wouldn't be seeing my Irish cowboy after that evening; but the next day, he called and asked if he could stop by the house. Donnie had answered the phone and told him, of course.

I didn't know he was arriving until someone said my name, and I jumped, turned around, and squirted Sean right in the face with the hose in my hand.

"Oh, I'm so sorry!" I turned the hose off and looked at our wet guest, and then, at myself. There I stood, in old cut-off shorts and a raggedy T-shirt that now was a wet T-shirt—revealing my too-snug bra and too-large breasts.

"Are you always a disaster, Miss Murphy?"

He took the towel I offered him.

I looked at his wet face, splotched chambray shirt and jeans, and started to laugh.

"I guess it seems that I am, huh?"

"Yes, it does. Can I help you with your car? Want me to do the inside?"

"Sure, if you want," I said, handing him the rags and inside cleaner.

We were nearly finished when Donnie came outside. "Hey, Sean! I wondered where you were." He looked from me to Sean.

"Lori! Did you squirt our guest?"

"Not on purpose," I said, feeling that flush rising up my neck.

"Mama always said Lori had to be one of the klutzy fairies from Ireland," Donnie said. "She's always been a disaster waiting to happen."

"Thanks, Donnie," I said. I picked up the hose and finished rinsing the car, then took a towel and started to wipe the water off the vehicle. Donnie got in one side, and Sean in the other, and finished cleaning the inside of my car.

"Y'all want some lunch?" I looked at Sean, whose clothes were beginning to dry, and he gave me a smile.

"Can you make cowboy beans and hotdogs?"

"Cowboy beans?"

"What? You've never heard of them?"

"Don't think so."

"There are a lot of versions of the recipe, but the one we made the most out on the trail, has ground beef, a green pepper, onion, salt and pepper, a can of baked beans, a can of Great Northern beans, ketchup, steak sauce, brown sugar, and Worchestershire sauce. If you have that stuff, I'll make them."

"How about some hotdogs and chips?"

I thought about all those other ingredients, and I knew I didn't have them.

"Sounds good to me," he said. "I'll make y'all the beans some other time."

Some other time? I wondered if that meant I'd be seeing him, again.

I did see Sean, again. In fact, I saw him everyday during the week he was home visiting. When he went back to Wyoming, we e-mailed, and called each other for the next few months. Then, he proposed to me on one of his trips home.

"Would you like to be buried with my people?" he asked.

"Would you like to hang your washing next to mine?" I asked.

Yes, this is the traditional Irish proposal!

"Tell ya what, Red, let's set a date to get married on Saint Patrick's Day. Seems that's what brought us, together."

"That's great. But do we have to serve green beer at the wedding?"

"Hey, that's a great idea! And maybe corned beef and cabbage for the dinner."

He chuckled when he watched my face.

"I think not!"

We had a great wedding with all the Irish traditions that I could find. I wore the lucky horseshoe on my wrist—made of fabric. We received several "make-up bells."

Those bells are to restore harmony if the couple is fighting, and to remind a couple of their wedding day.

Sean hired Irish dancers who passed out the programs before our wedding ceremony and later danced at the reception.

One of my friend's daughters sang the "Irish Wedding Song" at our wedding ceremony. And I carried a bouquet of Bells of Ireland. Each bridesmaid was presented with a sprig of live myrtle for them to plant. If it grew, the bridesmaid would marry within the year. And they were all single!

My mother told me I couldn't sing at my wedding because it would be bad luck. I promised her I wouldn't sing a note. She also informed me that I couldn't take both feet off the floor when I danced.

"If you do, Lori, the Fairies will get the upper hand. Fairies love beautiful things, and one of their favorites is a bride," she said. "There's many an Irish legend about brides being spirited away by the little people, and your Grandmother Murphy swore this was true."

Sean's mother refused for us to marry on a Saturday, which worked out fine since Saint Patrick's Day fell on a Sunday. "It's unlucky to marry on a Saturday," she said.

To my surprise, Sean's mother threw an old shoe over my head as we were leaving the church. She nearly clobbered me with it.

"Oops, sorry," she said. "I want you to have good luck."

And if that weren't enough, when we arrived at the reception, his mother had cut a piece out of our wedding cake, and broke it over my head.

"This means we'll always be friends," she said.

Sean's father had sent for Bunratty Meade wine from Ireland, which was served at Bunratty Castle for medieval banquets. He informed us that this was served at weddings because it was thought that it promoted virility.

"I think you'll be presenting us with a wee one nine months from now," he said, offering a toast.

I moved to Colorado with Sean, and true to his dad's word, we had our first baby nine months to the day of our wedding. Our baby girl was tiny, like a little fairy. So that's what we named her, Fairie Lorraine.

Although I liked Colorado and the clear blue skies, I missed Florida, my family, and friends something fierce.

"How would you like to move home?" Sean sat down on the sofa as he took Fairie and the bottle and fed her.

"I'd love it. Why?"

"I've been offered a transfer."

"Take it," I said.

We're back home, now, and I'm very happy with my Irish cowboy. And we just learned that we're going to have another Irish cowboy in two months.

Going to that party with my brother was the best thing I did for myself. That's where I met my love. He loved me in spite of my klutziness.

Sometimes, there really are happy endings!

THE END

# THE LUCK OF THE IRISH
## Tradition, Music, And A Handsome Man

My grandfather had come from Ireland to America, and my dad always told me that we had the luck of the Irish with us. He had no doubt that I would find a terrific man to marry when the time was right, just as he had found my mom. "It's the luck of the Irish, Colleen," he'd said time and again. As for me, at the age of thirty-two, I wasn't so sure. All of my friends were married and raising a family, while I was still single.

From the time I was a little girl, there was never a time I didn't know what my heritage was. In first grade, I remember the teacher asking us to find out what nationality our grandparents were, or what country they'd come from, for World Heritage day. When I told her I already knew, she seemed surprised.

"Well, Colleen, where did your grandparents come from?"

"From the Emerald Isle," I answered without hesitation.

"From Ireland?" she asked.

I nodded my head, beaming because my teacher knew that was Ireland.

"Yes, ma'am, my daddy told me his daddy called it the Emerald Isle 'cause everything's so green there. He told me no place in the world had fields and land so green. And on St. Patrick's Day, the leprechauns come and make our milk green, too."

That brought laughter from my classmates, and even the teacher had a huge smile on her face.

"Is that so?" she asked.

Nodding my head again, I returned her smile.

"Uh-huh and when Mama makes our mashed potatoes, they turn green from the milk."

Most of the kids laughed even harder, except for Lucy, my best friend.

"Wow," she said, "I wish the leprechauns would turn our milk green."

Then, the kids in my class got in on that idea, and some actually asked me to have "my" leprechaun come to their houses.

I smiled, remembering that long ago time. Maybe the memory had come to mind because it was just a few days till St. Patrick's Day, and Dad had been asking me if I'd go with him to the new Irish pub that had opened up in our town.

"It sounds like they know how to play an Irish tune, Colleen, and I'd love to hear some real Irish music, again. I've heard the drummer actually was born in Ireland and has only been here for a few years. It would be nice to talk to someone from the Emerald Isle, wouldn't it? I've asked your brothers and their wives to come along, too."

"Sure, Dad. Sounds like a fun way to spend St. Paddy's Day."

Inwardly, I sighed, wondering if this would be the way I would spend the holiday for the rest of my life: listening to Irish music with my family . . . and Dad as my date.

My father had turned seventy-four on his last birthday, but was as hearty as the rest of our Irish ancestors. I had no doubt he would live a long life.

When I'd come back home to live seven years ago, it was because my mom had cancer and needed special care. She wanted to spend her last weeks, or months—depending on which doctor you spoke to—at home, and I wanted to be there for her.

I'd moved out of state simply because I couldn't refuse the salary and perks I'd been offered as an E. R. nurse in Florida. But I'd missed home, and when Mom got sick, I felt I'd lost precious time with her.

Mom fooled all the doctors, though. Her will to live was stronger than they believed.

"It's because of the care you're giving her," Dad said after six months had passed. That made me feel better about the years I'd spent away from home—whether it was true or not.

For whatever reason, Mom rallied and lived for more than a year, with lots of good days . . . days spent talking and laughing and remembering.

I believe that year was given to me as a blessing. It became a time of such closeness between us, and I thanked God for it every day of my life. I grew closer to Dad, too, of course, as we talked long into the night after Mom would go to sleep.

When Dad asked me to stay at the house after Mom's funeral, I once again agreed, knowing he was devastated by the loss of the woman he'd loved so deeply.

The hospital where I'd first worked as a nurse was nearby and though the pay wasn't as good as it had been in Florida, I was home. My nieces and nephews loved having Auntie Colleen close by, too, and I enjoyed seeing their antics on a daily or weekly basis—rather than twice a year on vacation.

As weeks turned into months and months into years, it just seemed right to remain there with my father. I don't think he could have managed to keep the old house without my sharing expenses with him, and he did so love the place.

"It's where your mother and I raised all you children," he'd tell me when I broached the subject of selling it. "There are so many memories here, Colleen. I can't sell it, not yet."

39

As each of my friends married though, I grew more wistful, wondering when the man of my dreams would come along. Dad always reassured me that with the luck of the Irish in our family, I would find the perfect mate . . .

"When God sees fit," he'd add.

So, once again, I would be celebrating our family's most favorite day of the year with Dad as my "date."

My brothers and their wives would join us, if they could find a baby-sitter for their kids. Since I always enjoyed spending time with my family, I began to look forward to our evening, checking out the new Irish pub in our neighborhood.

Early on March 17th my youngest niece called with her "news."

"Aunt Colleen, the leprechaun was here. He turned our milk green, again. Did he come to Grandpa's and your house, too?"

"As a matter of fact, he did, sweetie. I had milk with my cereal this morning, and it was indeed green."

"The leprechauns like our family," she added, with a note of smug superiority that only six-year-olds can pull off.

"I believe they do. But be careful you don't brag about it too much. Sometimes, other people get upset because the leprechauns don't come to their house."

"Oh, I know. I only tell my best friends about it, and sometimes, Mom let's me invite them over to dinner so they can see our green mashed potatoes."

That brought a smile to my lips as I recalled having my friend, Lucy, over for dinner for the same reason. Now, thoughts of Lucy brought her happy life to mind. She had a wonderful husband who adored her and two little ones already, after only four years of marriage. So now, our roles were reversed and I envied her, as she had once envied my visit from the leprechaun. It wasn't truly envy, of course. I couldn't have been happier for my best friend. I just wanted to be happy too, and to be raising a family of my own.

By four o'clock, my brothers had both called. They and their wives would be joining us at Sullivan's Pub—after they fed their kids dinner.

"You know how they look forward to those green mashed potatoes," my brother said.

By six-thirty, our bellies were full of corned beef and cabbage and Irish beer.

"No green beer at this pub," the owner had told us. "That's purely an American thing. We import our beers from Ireland, and Guinness is my favorite."

So, we all had one to toast our Irish ancestors, then I switched to ginger ale, as I never was fond of beer. I would also be delegated to drive anyone home who overindulged on this special night.

Irish music played from speakers, but the promise of a "live" Irish band was what we were waiting for. They would come on at seven.

I saw him when the band started setting up. The muscles were hard to miss as he carried in their equipment. Maybe that's what I was staring at when he turned, and his blue eyes caught hold of mine. The intensity of his gaze held me fast.

By the time I blinked, breaking the connection, my heart hammered so hard I felt sure others could hear it.

His smile came then, and I smiled back. He was gorgeous, his dark hair falling in soft waves across a broad forehead—the smile illuminating his entire face.

He did a sort of salute, one finger to his forehead and toward me, then turned back to the equipment at the urging of one of the other band members.

My sister-in-law, Michelle, must have seen the exchange as she leaned over and said: "Now there's one good-looking guy, Colleen. If you're smart, you'll find a way to talk to him."

"Oh, come on," I said, "I'm not so hard up that I have to talk to a guy in a band."

"Of course not. You have guys calling you every week for dates. But, come on, he's a hunk, and he's the one in the band who's from Ireland. If nothing else, you need to introduce Dad to him, so they can talk about the Emerald Isle."

She said it with the inflection that most of the in-laws in the family did, often tired of hearing so much about the Irish heritage we came from.

After the second song, a love song poignantly sung by "blue eyes," I knew Michelle was right. I had to talk to that man.

They didn't take a break for a solid hour, and by then, I couldn't have walked away without talking to him. His voice had touched my heart.

I walked up to the stage, pulling Dad along behind.

"Hi, I'm Colleen Flannery, and this is my father, Patrick. We both wanted to compliment you on your vocals. Your voice brought Ireland to mind, and since my grandfather came from the Emerald Isle, it's been a joy to listen to your songs."

"Well I thank you, Colleen. I'm Kevin Malone, and I'm pleased to meet you and your father. Sir," he said, extending his hand to Dad. "It's my pleasure to meet someone whose ancestors come from my country."

"My father always spoke of the old sod, Kevin. And Colleen is right. You brought a bit of Ireland right here to our town, tonight."

"It's my pleasure to bring the old Irish tunes to those who appreciate hearing them. As for your daughter, sir," Kevin added,

41

turning his eyes toward me, "when I first came in, I noticed your lovely Colleen right away. She has the look of an Irish lass about her with the lovely red hair and green eyes befitting her heritage."

My face reddened at his compliment, and I was mortified, blushing at my age.

Dad was smiling, of course.

"Yes, she does. Her grandfather always told us we had a bit of Ireland right there in our own house."

I cleared my throat, still flustered by his calling me "lovely."

"We should let Kevin have his break, Dad. We can talk again later, if he has time."

"I have ten minutes right now, Colleen. Might I share a drink with you at your table? It seems you and your group know how to have a good time."

"That 'group' is all family," I said.

"Even better. A family who celebrates the old Saint's day together."

Before I knew it, Kevin was at our table, clinking a mug of Guinness with my brothers, asking Dad what part of Ireland we were from, and complimenting my sisters-in-law on being fine additions to our Irish family.

In ten minutes, he felt like an old friend.

Soon, he was back onstage, and the next love song he sang, seemed to come from his heart directly to mine. His eyes remained on mine for the entire song; and at the end, only loud applause from the crowd broke the bond between us.

At some point, my sisters-in-law went to the ladies room and asked me to join them. I didn't want to leave, but Michelle practically yanked me up from the table.

"Okay," she said, as we walked. "You have to invite him over for dinner. He's probably hungry for a good Irish meal, and you have all of your grandmother's recipes."

"Michelle, I can't invite a perfect stranger over for dinner."

"Why not?" Ian's wife asked. "Michelle's right. This is an opportunity you can't pass up. He is 'perfect,' but he's not a stranger, anymore. He's talked to all of us and shared a drink with your brothers. You need to jump on this, Colleen. I saw what went on between you during that last song. I believe he will accept the invitation. If he does turn you down, then it wasn't meant to be and Michelle and I are crazy."

"We're not crazy," Michelle added. "He will accept."

And he did. At the end of the evening, I suggested he might like to have an old-fashioned Irish meal, and he accepted—instantly.

Four days later, Kevin Malone was sitting at the dinner table with our entire family—including my five nieces and nephews. My sisters-in-law tried to weasel out of it, saying it would be better to have him all to myself, with Dad—of course. However, I wasn't about to sit there tongue-tied, as I knew I'd probably be with the man sitting across from me at the dinner table.

So there were twelve of us gathered together eating Irish stew and soda bread, recipes I'd taken right from my grandmother's recipe box.

Kevin talked to everyone, including all the kids. Everyone loved him, and despite the fact that I did not believe in love at first sight, I knew I'd fallen for him from that first glance on St. Patrick's Day.

He complimented me on everything I served, including the Irish coffee.

"Mr. Flannery, sir, you have quite a cook in this daughter of yours," he said. "Not to mention, she makes the best Irish soda bread I've had since leaving Ireland. No one in the States seems to have the knack of making it taste like home—except you, Colleen," he added, turning to me.

Again, his eyes reached in and touched me deep inside and I almost couldn't speak. Somehow, I formed a "thank you," and asked if he'd like more coffee.

"I'm full to the brim, actually," he answered. "What I truly need is a bit of a walk to allow me room for one more cup on our return . . . if you all wouldn't mind me stealing this lass away for a bit?"

His gaze traveled around the table, and smiles followed.

"You two go right ahead," Dad said. "Since Colleen did the cooking, we'll clear the table, and get the dishes done. When you get back, we'll all sit and have more coffee."

Moments later, Kevin and I were walking down the street I'd grown up on, talking as though we'd known each other, forever.

"Colleen," he said, after a couple of blocks. "It's so good to hear your voice. You barely spoke through dinner, and I was hoping I'd not misread the looks we've exchanged."

I had to smile at that.

"Oh, no, Kevin, you did not misread anything. I felt something special the first time our eyes met."

"So, is it your family that keeps you from speaking much?"

I shook my head.

"I can hold my own with my brothers and their families. Tonight, I was simply enjoying the sight of you relating to each of them. You weren't at all uncomfortable being surrounded by my brothers and their families. You connected with each of them, including every one of my nieces and nephews."

"And that's important to you?"

"Oh, yes. My family is very important to me, and there aren't many men who can handle the whole batch of them."

He laughed, and his laughter rippled over me like a lyrical ballad.

"Your clan is much like mine back home, sweet Colleen. Tonight was like being with family. Your father's home is warm and welcoming. Your brothers are men after my own heart. Their families remind me of my own sister's families.

"Yet, even if you had no family, even had we been alone at dinner, the warmth would still have been there. You are not only a beautiful women, but you have a special light in your eyes that touched me the night we met. When you came and introduced yourself, my heart truly leaped in my chest. I had been wondering how to go about meeting you, not wanting you to think I was one of those members of a band that make out with women at every place they play."

My pulse raced with each word he spoke till I was practically breathless.

"You wanted to meet me?"

"Oh, yes, from that very first moment, I knew we were destined to meet."

Destined. This man certainly had a way with words. And I was hanging on to every one of them.

As he finished that last sentence, he took my arms and turned me toward him—right there in the middle of town. His eyes held mine once more, and I knew without a doubt that he was going to kiss me.

His lips were gentle; yet, his kiss kindled a passion within that I'd never felt before—not in all the years since my first kiss at the age of fourteen.

"Kevin Malone," I said, breathlessly, ". . . are you aware that we are standing in the middle of town, with people walking by, looking at us?"

"Ah, yes indeed, lass. I'd have not trusted myself to kiss you if we'd been alone."

Unbelievably, those were the most romantic words I'd ever heard.

He smiled, took my hand in his, and headed back toward my home.

"Let's get back to your family, now," he said. "I believe we should all get to know each other better. I have a feeling we'll be seeing a lot of each other in the days to come."

"Me too," I said. "But I'm also looking forward to some more long walks with you, Kevin Malone . . . and some time alone, too."

Heading back home, with Kevin's hand in mine, I knew Dad had been right all along. The luck of the Irish was definitely on my side this time.

THE END

# ST. PATRICK'S DAY
# CHANGE OF HEART
## My Path To Finding Myself

"No, Stacey, I'm not going to the St. Patrick's Day party with you, and that's final," I said, firmly.

"C'mon, Joanie. You can't live your entire life in fear of that one night."

I glared back at my friend and shook my head.

"You obviously don't understand because you've never lost someone you love because some drunk driver was stupid enough to get behind a wheel."

"You're right," she said, softly, as she gently placed her hand on my shoulder. "I don't understand what that feels like. But I do understand one thing: Every single year since I've known you, all you do is sit at home and stare out the window on St. Patrick's Day, crying."

"But I loved my brother so much. He was my hero."

Tears stung the backs of my eyes, but I willed them not to fall.

"I know you looked up to him, but I don't think he'd want you to be miserable, Joanie."

I took a step back and sighed.

"I'm still not going out. You can find someone else who hasn't been through a tragedy on St. Patrick's Day."

Stacey left shortly after that. And I went to the spot where I did my best thinking—the window seat in my bedroom overlooking the road that led my older brother to his death seven years ago. To this day, I felt that familiar shiver of fear whenever St. Patrick's Day approached.

I'll never forget waiting up until nearly two a.m. for my brother, Jerome. He'd promised to bring me a shamrock from his favorite pub where they served green beer and green boiled eggs that one night every year. Jerome was really excited because he thought some really cute girl might be there.

My last words to him were to call home if he was too drunk to drive. He tousled my hair and said he wasn't stupid. He'd stop after two drinks. However, he never made it home because someone else had more than double the legal blood alcohol level, and he just happened to swerve into my brother's car. Jerome was less than a mile from home when it happened.

I heard the sirens, but at the time it didn't dawn on me that they were for my brother. I found myself hoping that whatever it was, wouldn't delay him from getting home before I went to bed. I was just seventeen, so anything he did at his ripe age of twenty-two, seemed so grown up and cool. About an hour later, as my annoyance grew, I saw the police officers pull up at the curb in front of our house. I couldn't imagine what they were doing here at this time of night.

Suddenly, I heard Mom scream and then hushed voices downstairs. I crept away from the window and went to see what was going on. Mom was crying, hysterically, her body heaving, while Dad held onto her, a look of stunned disbelief on his face. One of the police officers stood there watching as if he didn't know what to do. The other officer saw me and motioned for me to come over to them. I knew something was dreadfully wrong, and I sensed it had something to do with Jerome.

All I remembered hearing after that was, "Your brother died at the scene of the accident. He didn't know what hit him."

Over the next several months, we went to court, worked on getting the guilty man convicted of vehicular manslaughter and drunk driving, and learned everything we could about what had happened. The police informed us that in certain parts of the country, the most deadly night for drunk driving was St. Patrick's Day because of all the alcohol consumed.

So going out on St. Patrick's Day was totally out of the question for me. Not only did I want to stay out of harm's way on the deadliest traffic night of the year, I didn't want to celebrate the anniversary of the worst night of my life.

Stacey and I met a year later at the community college where she and I were in English composition class together. Both of us had Monday, Wednesday, and Friday classes, so we became lunch buddies. During the summer between our two years there, we hung out, and wound up being best friends. I loved Stacey like the sister I never had because she truly cared about me. She was willing to listen to stories about Jerome, and I listened to her talk about her parents' divorce—which had devastated her. We managed to remain close friends, even after we got our associate's degrees, and sometimes after work, we hung out at restaurants or went to movies.

My parents still grieved losing Jerome. In the days immediately following the tragedy, they were overly protective of me. However, over the past couple of years, they loosened up quite a bit and began to live their own lives, again. I saw Mom smile for the first time when Dad brought her a corsage on the night they went out for their thirtieth wedding anniversary.

I was jolted from my thoughts when I heard a knock at the door. I glanced up as Mom poked her head into my room.

46

"You okay, sweetie?" she asked. "When you didn't come down with Stacey, I thought maybe you were busy. But it's so quiet in here, I was worried."

"I'm fine. Just thinking."

I turned back around and looked out the window.

I heard the sound of her soft steps as she crossed the room and sat down beside me.

"I still think about him, too."

It's just so unfair for a young man with so much going for him to have it all end so suddenly."

The wistfulness in her voice undid me. I wasn't able to keep the tears from falling, now. Mom reached for my hand, squeezed it, then let go.

"But you can't stop enjoying life, Joanie. Jerome loved his life, and he loved his family. He wouldn't have wanted you to sit around and not go anywhere."

"I go places," I argued.

"Maybe you physically go out once in a while, but I don't see you having any fun. Stacey said she invited you to join her at a St. Patrick's Day party. Why don't you go?"

I gasped as I turned and faced my mother.

"How can you say that after what happened? That police officer said St. Patrick's Day evening was the most dangerous night on the road."

"And that's why they've stepped up patrol. I heard they've more than doubled the number of officers on duty that night. Really, Joanie, it's much safer now than it was."

"I still don't want to celebrate," I said. "It's just not right."

"Jerome would have grabbed you by the hair and dragged you to that party," Mom argued. "He would never want you to miss a great party."

"What are you and Dad doing?" I asked.

She shrugged.

"We're having a few friends over to play cards. Why don't you go be with some people your own age, and at least try to have some fun?"

"I'll think about it," I replied, more than anything to get her to leave me alone. I really didn't feel like arguing over something I felt so strongly about.

Mom and Dad nagged me until I finally agreed to go out with Stacey. But I never agreed to like it.

Stacey giggled with delight when she picked me up.

"Trust me, Joanie," she said, "we'll be just fine." She made an issue of clicking her seatbelt and said, "See? All buckled up. My car has airbags, and I'll stay off the high traffic roads if that makes you feel better."

I shrugged.

"It doesn't matter. Jerome was in a residential area when he was hit. Drunk drivers can be anywhere."

47

Her shoulders drooped, and she gave me a look that let me know she was annoyed.

"Look. Tonight is supposed to be fun. I plan to have fun, and I want you to try your best to have a good time. The limit at the party is one drink per hour, and some people won't even have that."

I swallowed hard. It was difficult not to say what was on my mind—that the person who plowed into my brother wasn't at the same party as him—but I didn't. I kept it to myself because I didn't want to make my friend mad.

We were among the first to arrive at Hayden's house. He was standing outside on his front porch waving us into his double car driveway.

"The first four groups here get the best spots," he said. "And y'all are the third."

Stacey grinned ear to ear and nudged me as we walked up the sidewalk leading to the front door.

"See? The night's starting off good, already. This is going to be a fun party, whether you like it or not."

I made my way inside and found the table stocked with munchies. Stacey had brought a couple of platters of sandwiches, and she added them to the table.

"Why didn't you tell me I needed to bring food?" I asked.

She waved me off.

"Don't worry about it. I figured you were doing good just to come. No point in adding another reason for you to change your mind."

"Hey, gorgeous!" I heard from behind. I swirled around in time to see Andy from the accounting department at the company where Stacey worked. I'd seen him several times, and Stacey said he liked me. "You didn't tell me you'd be here!"

"I didn't know I was coming until last night," I admitted.

"This is the best party in town," he said. "Last year, I got so dru—"

Stacey cut him off and led him away.

"I wanna show you my car, Andy."

"Did you get new wheels?"

I knew exactly what she was doing, and I loved her for it. Andy didn't have a clue about what I'd been through with drunk drivers, so Stacey no doubt planned to set him straight. I'd always thought Andy was sort of cute, but he didn't always know the right things to say. Stacey said that was part of his charm in the office, and everything treated him like a little brother for that very reason.

Hayden came to my side and offered me a drink.

"We have soda if you don't want beer, wine, or any of the hard stuff."

"I'll take ginger ale if you have it," I said.

"One green ginger ale coming right up."

He handed me a green napkin-covered glass, filled with sparkling green liquid and a bright green straw. I tilted my head back and laughed.

"Where did you get all the green stuff?"

"It's not hard this time of year. Can I get you anything else?"

I leaned forward and glanced at the table that by now was groaning with an abundance of food.

"I might have a sandwich in a few minutes."

Some more people came in, so he left me to greet them. I glanced around to see where Stacey had gone. She was nowhere in sight, but I spotted Andy as he made a beeline to me.

"Hey, Joanie, I'm really sorry about acting like a jerk. Stacey told me what happened to your brother. That's a tough thing to deal with."

"Yeah, it's really hard."

He gently placed his hand on my arm and turned me around to face him. "I want you to know that I passed out on the floor last year. I didn't drive home drunk. I wouldn't do something like that, but even if I wanted to, Hayden wouldn't have let me. He's very conscientious about keeping his guests—and everyone else on the road—safe."

"That's nice."

"Seriously," he said. "You know what he does for a living, right?"

I shook my head. I'd only met Hayden once, and that was when Stacey and I had gone out one dateless Friday night.

"I have no idea."

"He's a police detective."

"You're kidding." I squinted as I looked back over at Hayden. "He doesn't look like a cop."

Andy chuckled.

"And I don't look like an accountant, do I?"

Honestly, he did, but he clearly didn't want me to think so. I shook my head.

"Not really."

"What do I look like?" he asked, openly flirting with me. "Be truthful."

Thankfully, Stacey came to my rescue.

"You look like Andy, that's who," she said.

We all laughed. I had to admit, I was having a really nice time. I was glad Stacey had talked me into coming to the party.

One of the guys I met that evening asked if I wanted to dance. I took a step back and said, "Not now. Maybe later."

He tilted his head to one side.

"It's just a dance."

"I know, but I'm not ready to dance, yet."

With his hands raised in surrender, he walked away.

49

"It's not like I was asking for a lifelong commitment or anything. Sheesh!"

Stacey sidled up to me a few minutes later, her eyes sparkling with delight.

"Still having fun?" she asked.

I shrugged.

"Yeah, I guess."

"I brought you here, but I can't make you have a good time. Lighten up. Talk to people. Dance. This is a party!"

"I know, but you do realize what a big step this was for me. Just give me some time, okay?"

She nodded her head toward Hayden who was chatting with a couple of people in the opposite corner of the room.

"Hayden thinks you're cute."

"Really? What did he say?"

"He just asked about you. Last time he saw you, he didn't get a good look at you."

"Yeah, I remember he was also in a big hurry. He said he was meeting some people, and he was running late."

Stacey stepped in front of me, which forced me to face her.

"Joanie, don't let this big opportunity get away from you. I know it's a big step for you to even be here, but that's all the more reason to step out of your comfort zone a little more and get to know some really nice people."

"It's just so hard," I argued.

"I know it's hard. Your brother must have been one heck of a guy. You loved him so much, and he clearly loved you, too—based on what all you've said about how he always brought you surprises."

"We were as close as a brother and sister can be."

"Do you think he'd want you standing around being a wallflower?"

"Well, no. . . . "

"What would Jerome have done if he'd come to this party?" she asked.

I squirmed.

"I don't know."

"Yes, you do. You know exactly what he'd be doing. He'd be right in the middle of the action, telling jokes, dancing, and charming all the ladies."

"How would you know?" I asked.

"Because you told me that's what he did."

"Oh, yeah," I said. "But we were different."

"I think you can be as charming as your brother was. When I met you, I remembered feeling scared at the community college because I didn't know anyone. You came up to me and asked me what classes

50

I had. If it hadn't been for you doing that, I'm not sure I would have lasted the whole two years."

"Really?"

"Really. You're one of the friendliest people I've ever met, but no one would believe me based on how you're standing here practically daring anyone to come near you."

"Is that what I'm doing?" I asked.

"That's exactly what you're doing."

My mind was swirling with all she'd just said, but I knew she was right. I was at a party, so I might as well make the most of it.

"I'll do my best to have fun, okay?" I said.

"That's all I can ask. Now, next time someone asks you to dance, say yes."

"I can't dance."

"Anyone can dance. Just move to the music."

I started to argue with her, but she turned and flitted off to chat with a couple who just entered the room. I stood there trying to figure out what to do first.

"That's some wild looking juice you're drinking," some guy I'd never seen before said. "Want me to get you a refill?"

I quickly glanced around the room, hoping someone would rescue me. My gaze caught with Andy's. He took the unspoken hint and was by my side in a split second.

"Hey, Joanie, ready to dance?" Andy asked, as he did some silly footwork.

I tilted my head back and laughed.

"I'm not sure I can keep up with you, Andy."

The guy who'd been standing there stepped in front of Andy.

"I saw her first, buddy; so scram!"

My heart pounded. I didn't like the sound of what was happening. However, it didn't go any further. Next thing I knew, Hayden was right there, in the guy's face.

"Hey, Dave, what's happening? Are you having fun?"

"Uh, yeah, I'm having a great time. I was just about to ask this hot chick to dance with me."

Hayden glanced at me before quickly turning back to the guy he called Dave.

"I don't think the lady wants to dance with you."

"Oh, I'm sure—"

Without giving the guy a chance to finish his sentence, Hayden physically turned him completely around and pointed.

"See that pretty lady over there? She's been watching you all evening. If you don't mess up, she just might dance with you, among other things."

"Cool."

Dave had forgotten all about me as he walked across the room toward the woman Hayden had pointed toward.

"Thanks," I said.

"Just making sure all my guests behave," Hayden replied, before backing away.

I wanted to talk to him more, but he clearly took his hosting responsibilities very seriously.

"Now, would you like to dance?" Andy said.

Before I had a chance to think too much about it, I nodded and took his arm.

"I'd love to. Just don't laugh when I trip all over myself. I haven't danced in years."

"It's not hard. Just do what I do."

After watching him making all kinds of crazy moves on the makeshift dance floor, I tilted my head back and laughed.

"I'm afraid I'd injure myself if I did all that."

"I'm happy to see you, smiling," Hayden said as he edged up beside me and handed me another glass of ginger ale. "I've only seen you once before, and I thought it would be nice to get to know you better."

Suddenly, I felt all warm inside. I liked Hayden. He was a fun, comfortable guy to be around, and I never felt like his flirting was over the top or out of line. He had an amazing way of making me feel like the only other person in the room.

"Thank you," I said. "This is one of the nicest parties I've ever been to."

He grinned.

"That's because I only have the nicest people at my parties. I learned something a long time ago. If I want to have a good time and make sure everyone stays in line, I have to be the host where I can call the shots."

"Good point," I said.

"Take a look around," he said, gesturing toward the crowd. "Do you see a single drunk person in the room?"

I glanced out at everyone and saw that no one was staggering or slurring their words.

"Not even one."

"They know the rules coming in here. One drink per hour, and even at that, they have to pass my inspection before they get their car keys back."

I turned and faced him, squinting.

"You took their car keys?"

"Yep. I have them locked away in a safe place. I don't want to be responsible for anyone leaving my party and getting hurt—or hurting someone else." He paused before adding, "I also go out to their cars with them and make sure they have their seatbelts on."

I remembered that there had been some question about whether or not Jerome would have survived if he'd had his seatbelt buckled. Mom used to fuss at us all the time, reminding us to "buckle up for safety," whenever we left the house. Most of the time I remembered, but Jerome said it cramped his style.

Hayden turned me around to face him, and gently tilted my face up so he could see it.

"Did I say something wrong?"

I shook my head.

"No."

"What happened to you just now? You look like you suddenly went into your own little zone."

Obviously, he didn't know about my brother, so I figured I might as well tell him, or he'd think my mood was his fault.

"Several years ago," I began, "my brother, Jerome, left the house to go to a St. Patrick's Day party." Pain shot through me, but I managed to keep talking. "He had a couple of drinks, but he was responsible. He didn't believe in driving drunk. Anyway, I was too young to go to parties where there was drinking, so I waited up to listen to how much fun he had. I did that all the time." By now, my voice was cracking. I reached up and swiped at my tear-stained cheek with the back of my hand.

"Did something happen?" he asked, softly.

With a nod, I replied, "Jerome never made it back home. He was hit by a drunk driver."

Hayden's jaw tightened, and he hung his head.

"I am so sorry, Joanie. I had no idea. Now, I understand why you got so quiet. I shouldn't have pressed for answers."

"Don't worry about it. You didn't know."

"When I have a party at my house, safety is my first issue," he reminded me. "And a good time, is my second. I don't want anyone here to go home without a smile on their face."

"Trust me, Hayden, I'll have a smile on my face when I go home, tonight."

He looked into my eyes and held his gaze for almost a minute.

"I'd like to see that smile after tonight."

My heart thudded.

"That would be nice."

"Will you be here for a while?" he asked.

I nodded.

"I'll stay until Stacey's ready to leave."

"Good. We can chat after I make the rounds, again. In the

meantime, have some more ginger ale and another sandwich or two."

I chuckled.

"I've already consumed more calories tonight than I should in an entire week."

He looked me over and gave me a thumbs-up.

"You look great to me. Don't worry about calories, tonight. Just eat whatever you want, and dance it off."

As soon as he left my side, Stacey was right there.

"Looks like you've made a serious impression on our host."

"He's very nice."

She quirked an eyebrow and gave me a knowing look.

"C'mon, admit it. He's more than nice. He's the kind of guy you want to bring home to meet the parents."

"Okay, okay," I admitted. "You're absolutely right."

"Did he ask you to go on a date?"

"Not yet, but I think he's going to." I leaned forward to see where he was, and I caught him looking right back at me. I waved and turned back to Stacey. "I am so glad you talked me into coming."

"See? Going out on St. Patrick's Day isn't so bad, is it?"

"No, but I'm sure I'll always think about my brother."

Her expression grew solemn.

"I can understand that. Something would be wrong with you if you didn't. But also think about the kind of guy he was. Based on what I've heard from you and other people who knew him, he really knew how to have fun."

"Yes, he did," I said with conviction.

"And I think it's time I learned how to have fun, too."

"Atta girl," she said. "C'mon, we're gonna go dance."

"By ourselves?" I asked.

"It doesn't matter. Just move to the music and have fun!"

For the rest of the evening, I allowed myself to get caught up in the festive mood. When most of the guests had passed Hayden's inspection and left, he cornered me with a pen and paper.

"Write down your phone number, and I'll call. Maybe we can go out to dinner and a movie next weekend."

I did what he said and handed the paper back to him.

"I'm really looking forward to it."

"Me, too," he said, before he bent over and dropped a soft kiss on my cheek. I shivered. I loved feeling desirable.

All the way home, Stacey and I chattered on and on about the party and how much fun we had.

"Do you realize how many girls are interested in Hayden?" she said.

"I can only imagine. He's cute, sweet, smart, and very protective."

I sighed as I settled back in my seat.

As we passed the intersection where my brother was killed, the old familiar sadness crept over me. But this time, I didn't let my thoughts control me. I shut my eyes and said a prayer that I'd be able to deal with the pain better than I had been. I knew Jerome wouldn't have wanted me to be the sad person I'd become. He would have wanted me to grieve for a little while, but then he would have said to move on.

Now, St. Patrick's Day has a double meaning in my life. It's the anniversary of losing my brother, but it's also the anniversary of finding myself!

THE END

# IRISH EYES ARE SMILING
## Now That I've Found Love

"How's it look?" Fran asked me as she finished hanging the last shamrock over the reception desk.

The decorations depressed me, but I said, "You've done a great job."

Fran climbed down from her chair and stood back to admire her handiwork. She'd tastefully decorated the dental office lobby with shamrocks, leprechauns, and St. Patrick's Day garland. To our patients, the lobby would be cheery and reflect the holiday only days away. To me, the decorations were depressing, but then I was probably the only person in the world who was depressed about St. Patrick's Day.

Before this year, St. Patrick's Day had been my favorite holiday. My family always had a family party on the holiday. I loved the Irish dishes my mother prepared. The love and fun I shared with my family and friends made the day even more special. The holiday meant so much to my family and me that I had planned to announce my engagement to Seth Edison at this year's party. My dad had asked my mom to marry him on St. Patrick's Day, so I thought it would be sweet to announce my engagement on that day.

About a month ago all of my plans changed. Seth and I were having dinner at his brother's house when Seth's nephew, Gavin, started talking to us. This was the first time I'd really seen Seth interact with a child. I loved children, so I thought it would be fun for Seth and me to talk with Gavin. Instead, I was horrified by Seth's behavior toward nephew. Seth acted like a bully; he was mean to Gavin.

When I mentioned Seth's behavior to him on the way home, he shrugged off my concerns. "You have to show kids who's the boss, otherwise they won't stay in line. Besides, I was mostly teasing." But it didn't feel like teasing to me. Judging from Gavin's sad eyes and quivering lower lip, he didn't take Seth's comments lightly, either.

After several long discussions with Seth about children, I knew I couldn't marry him. I didn't even like him anymore. I was also mad at myself for not learning all aspects of Seth's personality before I got engaged.

When I saw the smiling leprechauns and bright shamrocks decorating the office, all I could think of was how stupid I'd been to even think of marrying Seth.

"Roger bought all of these things for the office," Fran said,

56

breaking into my thoughts. "He even asked me to hang some of the shamrocks in the treatment rooms."

Roger was a new dentist that had joined Valley Dental Group right before Christmas. He specialized in pediatric dentistry.

"He's one of the few men in the world that are both nice and good-looking," Fran said. "He'd be a nice guy for you."

I met Fran's gaze and laughed softly. "We don't even know each other. Besides, he probably has a girlfriend."

Fran pursed her lips and shook her head. "No girlfriend. I overheard him saying that he'd broken up with someone a few months ago and wasn't seeing anyone."

I was glad we were talking in hushed tones at the receptionist desk, because Roger strode into the lobby while Fran was still telling me how wonderful he was. Roger was wearing chocolate brown pants, a pale blue shirt, and a tie with cartoon characters on it. Fran had told me that he liked to put his young patients at ease, so he dressed casually and usually wore fun ties.

"The lobby looks great." Roger stood near the reception desk and gazed around the room. He was standing close enough for me to feel the warmth of his body and breathe in the scent of his cologne. My pulse began to race and my heart skipped a beat. I was all too aware of the handsome man standing inches from me.

"We need a shamrock plant for the counter. Or maybe some green carnations. What do you think?" Roger turned his gaze to me.

I was still unnerved by his closeness, and I fumbled for words. "Either would be nice. Green carnations are my favorite."

"Green carnations are romantic," Fran said. She smiled from ear to ear.

"Carnations are special," Roger said. "I'll go to the florist at lunch and get something."

The entrance door swung open and Bill Houston, one of our longtime patients, walked in. Bill was my first patient of the day. I was glad to have an excuse to get away from the lobby. My heart was still skipping.

"I'll be right with you, Bill," I said as I took advantage of my chance to escape.

I smiled at Roger and Fran, who were still talking at the reception desk, and headed down the hallway to make sure the treatment room was ready for Bill. Shamrocks and leprechauns danced along the hall to the treatment rooms.

I was still confused by my reaction to Roger in the lobby. That brief encounter was the most conversation I'd had with him. I didn't know what was wrong with me. Usually I could talk smoothly no matter who was around. I must've been embarrassed because Roger appeared when Fran and I were talking about him.

I'd been introduced to Roger when he joined the practice, and we always exchanged greetings when we saw each other, but I'd never really talked with him. I was Dr. Browne's dental hygienist, so I never went into the wing where Roger treated his patients.

I noticed Roger in the office, of course. He was hard not to notice. Besides his colorful ties, there were his natural good looks. Roger was good-looking in a warm and caring way. He always had a smile on his face. He looked like someone who'd be loyal and caring. There was a certain sexiness about him, too. I'd noticed it from a distance before, but this morning I'd experienced the power of his masculinity.

He was certainly making the most of St. Patrick's Day. As much as I didn't like the decorations this year, I had to admit it was kind of him to bring them into the office. A lot of guys wouldn't do that. I tried to put Roger out of my mind and concentrate on my patients, but I couldn't because my senses wouldn't let me forget how I'd felt standing close to him at the reception desk.

I lingered at work that night because I was in no hurry to get to my parents' house. My mother had asked my brother, Doug, and me to dinner so we could discuss the St. Patrick's Day party. I knew Mom and Dad would be energized about the party and would want to talk about every aspect of the celebration in great detail. It was exactly what I didn't want to do.

The lobby was dark and the building was quiet as I walked by the reception desk. Even in the darkness I couldn't help noticing a large shamrock plant wrapped in bright green foil sitting on the counter. It was probably from Roger, since he'd said he was going to pick up something at the florist. As much as I didn't need any more holiday reminders, a part of me wished that Roger had bought green carnations since I'd said they were my favorite.

Suddenly, there was pounding on the front door. Through the glass door I could see a woman and a small boy. The boy's face was bloody, and he was shrieking. The woman didn't look much better. She had blood on her hands and was babbling. I unlocked the door.

"Matt fell and hit his mouth. I think some teeth broke." The woman paused and gazed down at the boy. "There's so much blood."

"It probably looks worse than it is," Roger said as he walked up to us. Thank goodness he was still in the office. The building was so quiet that I was afraid I was on my own.

"Come on back and tell me what happened." He put his arm around the boy's shoulders and steered him down the hall. Roger turned and motioned for the mother to follow. I whipped off my coat, threw it on a chair, and followed them down the hall.

"What's your name?" Roger asked the boy as he helped him off with his coat and settled him in the dental chair.

"Matt."

"This is my friend." Roger held up a small brown teddy bear. The boy's crying paused as his blue eyes gazed at the bear. "He's looking for a home, and I told him you would take him with you. Can you do that?"

The boy nodded.

"And you'll give him a name, too?" Roger's eyes never left Matt's face as he talked.

Matt nodded again.

Roger's face broke out into a big smile. "Good, that's settled then. I'll put the bear over here so you can see each other." He put the bear on the edge of the counter where Matt could see it no matter what position the chair was in.

While Roger talked with Matt's mother about what had happened, I went through Roger's drawers and cupboards looking for supplies and instruments. I cleaned up Matt's face and hands and put a bib around his neck. I set out a tray with some instruments I thought Roger might need. I hadn't done chairside assisting in years, so my skills were rusty. I also didn't know Roger's procedures and the specific instruments that he most often used. I was doing my best, but I was still afraid Roger would think I was incompetent.

"Would you please show Matt's mother to the lobby? Then we'll take a look at Matt," Roger said to me. Then he turned to Matt's mother. "The lobby's more comfortable and it's decorated for St. Patrick's Day." He discussed the decorations like we were the only place in town with the theme. He must have really liked the holiday.

I showed Matt's mother to the lobby and gave her our new patient forms to fill out, and then went back to help Roger. He already had the exam light on, and Matt's mouth was open. As he gently explored Matt's injuries he talked to the young boy about the bear, the cartoon figures on his tie, and the shamrocks hanging from the ceiling.

"Looks like you knocked one of your baby teeth loose," Roger said when he was done with the exam.

Matt's eyes grew round, and he looked thoughtful. "Will it fall out?"

"Eventually, but I think I should help it along so you don't have to worry about it. Is that okay with you?"

Matt nodded slowly.

"And after we're done you'll take my bear home. Right?"

Matt nodded more vigorously this time.

"I'll go talk to your mom while Rebecca gets things ready."

I wanted to get things ready, but I felt like a klutz. My mind went blank as I struggled to remember procedures and instruments that I hadn't been familiar with in years.

As though reading my mind, Roger came over to me. "I know you don't know where things are kept. Find what you can. I'll get the rest when I come back."

He's nice to children and adults, I thought as I pulled out drawers, looking for instruments.

"I'll clean the instruments," I said as I picked up the tray with the used instruments. Roger had removed Matt's loose tooth, and the boy had left the office with his new bear gripped tightly in his hand.

Roger shook his head. "No, that's fine. You've done enough." He took the tray from my hand and carried it into the workroom.

"I'm afraid I'm a little out of practice," I said as I followed him. More than once I'd handed him the wrong instrument, or I'd gotten in the way.

"Believe me, your help was appreciated, and you did great." He set down the tray and leaned against the counter so he could face me. His gaze met mine. "I hope I didn't keep you from anything you had planned."

I shook my head. "I'm going to my parents' house to discuss our St. Patrick's Day plans, and I still have plenty of time to get there." If anything, I was glad not to be early.

"What does your family do for the holiday?"

I told him about our annual family party. "Mom does all of the cooking," I said.

"Does she make Irish soda bread?"

I nodded and smiled.

"And shepherd's pie?" His eyes were dancing as he named the meat and potato pie.

I nodded again.

"My mom was Irish. Unfortunately, all of her cooking secrets went to Heaven with her. My sister's a good cook, but she can't make Irish food like Mom did." He talked some more about his mother and how he missed her. "St. Patrick's Day was her favorite holiday. I guess that's why I like to decorate for the day. I feel like I'm doing something for her."

His eyes clouded for a moment, then he smiled and pushed away from the counter. "Time for you to get going to your party planning." He wrapped his arm around my shoulders and walked with me to the lobby. He picked up my coat from the chair and held it out so I could slip it on.

I couldn't remember when anyone had helped me with my coat. The gesture was nice, but what I liked most was the feel of Roger's hands on my shoulders as I slipped my arms into the sleeves. I could feel the heat of his body against my back, and small ripples of pleasure ran down my spine.

As I drove to my parents' house I replayed the last hour through my mind. I tried to ignore the physical sensations that Roger's touch had sent through my body and concentrated on his personality. Roger was really good with children. He was considerate of their parents, too. I remembered how he'd calmed Matt's mother. He was also patient with dental hygienists who were doing their awkward best at chairside assisting. Fran was right—he was good looking and nice. He was the kind of man I would like in my life.

I needed to come to my senses. I'd hardly said two words to Roger until today, now my heart raced just thinking about him. I was feeling romantic about ordinary events. Such thinking was a good way to get hurt. I continued listing all the reasons I shouldn't be interested in Roger until I saw the lights of my parents' house, and I turned into their driveway.

"Emergency? What kind of emergency?" Mom stopped mashing potatoes when I told her I was late because we'd had an emergency at the office. Across the kitchen I could see Dad's ears perk up, and Doug giving me a brotherly stare.

I explained about Matt and how I'd helped Roger. I couldn't help telling them that Roger's mother was Irish and he missed her cooking.

My words were hardly out of my mouth when Mom said, "You should invite him to our party."

I shook my head. "We hardly know each other." Now I wished I hadn't told them so much about Roger. They probably thought I liked him. Not that I didn't—I was just confused about my feelings.

"I know this year's party isn't working out like you'd planned," Mom said. "Inviting Roger may be a way to make you feel better."

"I can't ask him for a date," I said.

"A date?" Mom shook her head and frowned. "You kids make too big of a deal out everything these days. Just ask him for dinner. It sounds like he'd enjoy himself."

I managed to change the subject, but the idea of asking Roger to the party kept popping into my mind as I ate dinner.

The next day when I walked into the lobby, Fran met me with a smile on her face. "I heard you had some excitement after the office closed last night. Roger told me how helpful you were."

"He did?" My voice was a whisper. I didn't want Roger to catch us talking about him again. "I was so clumsy." I told Fran about some of my goofs and mistakes.

"He didn't mention any of those things. He said that you dove right in and helped him when he needed someone."

"Did you know his mother was Irish?" I asked.

Fran nodded. "He mentioned that when he brought in the decorations. I think he misses her at this time of year."

"My mom thinks I should invite him to our party."

Fran's face burst into a big smile. "That's a great idea."

"I'm not so sure. I'm still thinking about it." I'd thought about it all night and on the way to work.

"You'd better hurry and ask him. Tomorrow's St. Patrick's Day,"

Fran said as she reached for the ringing phone.

I walked down the hall to my work area. Today the shamrocks and leprechauns in the hallway didn't bother me so much. I looked at them not so much as my own personal failure, but as a man's way of remembering his mother. Roger seemed to be the sentimental type.

The day was unusually busy. One of my early appointments was late, which threw my timing off for all of my patients. As I worked, I kept weighing the pros and cons of asking Roger to the party. To begin with, how would I do it?

I couldn't barge into his treatment rooms and ask him. If I asked to talk to him privately his assistants would wonder what was going on and I'd feel awkward. Besides, I didn't have any time for making dates. I was too busy tying to catch up on my appointments.

By the end of the day, I was so tired all I wanted was a hot bubble bath and a glass of white wine. The party and Roger were still on my mind, though. Perhaps I'd see him on my way out of the office. As I passed the reception desk I could see the children's wing was dark.

"Is everyone gone?" I asked Fran.

She nodded. "Roger, too. Did you talk to him?"

"No, I hardly had time to talk to my patients today." I gave a weary sigh.

"There's always tomorrow," she said. Her encouraging smile matched the tone of her voice.

Asking him tomorrow seemed tacky, like a last-minute gesture. I'd probably embarrass myself by asking him, anyway. What if he turned me down? Then I would've created an uncomfortable situation for both of us.

The phone was ringing when I walked into my apartment. It was Mom. "Is Roger coming?" She sounded like she assumed that he was.

As I struggled out of my coat, I explained about my day and how I hadn't had time to breathe.

"Ask him tomorrow morning then," Mom explained.

"This probably isn't a good year," I said. "I'm really not in the party mood."

"Rather than thinking about what the party might have been, you should be thinking how wonderful the party could be."

Mom always saw the bright side, and I knew she wanted me to lift my spirits. "I'm sure I'll have a good time once the party gets going," I said.

"That's not what I meant," her voice rose over the phone. "Think of other ways to make the party special this year. Like bringing a man who hasn't had good Irish cooking since his mother died. Think of making his day special, not yours. Believe me, you do that and you'll be surprised how good you'll feel."

Mom's words made sense, but I still didn't think I wanted to gamble with Roger turning me down. Mom and I talked some more, and then I hung up.

I poured myself a glass of wine, went into the bathroom, and started filling the tub. The lavender-scented bubbles teased my nose as I leaned back against my tub pillow. But all I could think of was the musk of Roger's cologne and his brown eyes.

The next afternoon I was gathering up my instruments after cleaning a patient's teeth when Roger poked his head into the treatment room. He was wearing a bright green shirt, and a white tie with green shamrocks. I couldn't help smiling when I saw him.

"Like it?" he asked as he held out his tie and smiled.

"Very much in the holiday spirit," I said.

"I stopped by to thank you for helping the other night. I came by several times yesterday, but I could see that you were busy."

"I was glad I could help. You were great with Matt. I know he liked the bear."

"I've discovered that having stuffed animals on hand is a good way to help when kids are really over the edge."

Our gazes met and held for a moment.

"Well, I've got work to do," he said. He smiled and swung toward the hallway.

"Roger."

He stepped back into the room.

I took a deep breath. "I know it's short notice, but I was wondering if you'd like to come to my family's St. Patrick's Day party tonight."

"With the shepherd's pie and Irish soda bread?" His eyes were smiling as he teased me.

I nodded.

"Yes, I'd love to come. I was hoping you'd ask me."

This year's St. Patrick's Day party was the best of my life. The greatest joy was being with Roger. With him at my side, every aspect of the party came to life. Mom's holiday dishes tasted better than ever; my uncle's tired jokes sounded new; and my dad's singing wasn't so flat. Mom was right about how good a person feels by doing something special for someone. The smile in Roger's eyes as he sat with a plate full of food and told stories about his mother warmed my heart and soul.

Every once in a while I'd glance at the table where I'd placed the bouquet of green carnations that Roger had brought me. When he handed them to me I was so surprised all I could say was, "I like green carnations."

He smiled and with a husky voice and said, "I know. They're romantic."

THE END

# THE SQUIRREL AND
# THE LEPRECHAUN
The Squirrel Was Average– Even Ordinary–
But The Leprechaun Was Six Feet Tall
And Handy Around The House!

Outside, a cold spring rain poured down and the blustery wind whipped around my house. It was mid-March and the heater was clanking away—one more thing falling apart and one more bill to go unpaid. I thought of the beer that I'd bought the week before to celebrate the holiday: St. Patrick's Day. The six-pack still sat in my fridge because I didn't feel like celebrating.

The day before, my boss announced that my department was being outsourced, meaning that someone in another country would be doing my job. I had accrued vacation pay and was given one day to pack up my office. My ten-year stint with the company was over.

In the hours since my boss's announcement, I had done nothing but worry. I had hardly eaten and I couldn't sleep. I imagined all the worst possibilities. I pictured myself homeless and with nothing to eat, unable to find another job. I'd lose the house my husband and I bought twenty years ago and my car, a two-year-old Honda, would be repossessed. I'd be living on the streets. I just knew that the worst of all possible scenarios was bound to happen.

When I told my children about getting fired, they immediately offered their homes and invited me to stay with them until things had smoothed out. My daughter, Kathleen, and her husband, Ryan, were the parents of my two grandchildren and I'd like nothing more than to spend some time with them but I couldn't do it just yet. My pity party wasn't over and I wasn't good company for anyone.

My son, Steve, wasn't married and had only recently accepted his first job after graduation. He works in a bank and his life is just getting started. He didn't need me intruding, dumping my problems in his lap. I needed to try to handle it, just like I handled most everything since their father died more than five years ago. Eventually I would; I had to get over my depression first.

I told them I had a busy weekend ahead of me and then I stayed home. Actually, my calendar was empty. I rarely saw the people that I considered to be my friends. I poured myself into my job after Cole died and worked more than sixty hours each week as a secretary at an accounting firm. It had been months since I had done anything socially with anyone. Now that I was finally going to have time again, I couldn't think of anything I wanted to say to my friends—or anything I might want to do with them. What did we have in common now? I was unemployed and middle-aged. I weighed too much and my hair was turning gray. What did I have to offer anyone? What hope was there for my future? My self-pity poured down inside me like the rain outside the wide windows of my little house on the edge of a national forest.

This morning my sister, Megan, called and asked me to meet her in a nearby town to go antiquing for the day. I even said no to that invitation. My excuse had been the rain, which had been pouring down for hours and was supposed to continue all day. Much simpler to stay here, bundled in a thick, woolen Irish sweater my mother had brought me after her last visit to the home country thirty years ago.

I was depressed. Probably the last thing I needed was to be stuck in this house alone on a rainy St. Patrick's Day. Outside, the rain poured down. I opened the French doors that went out to the covered patio and left them ajar, letting the scent of rain waft into the house on the fresh spring air.

I kicked around the house trying to find something useful to do to get my mind off this situation. In reality, I felt like curling up on the sofa and going to sleep. I found myself thinking that it would be nice if I never woke up.

Something drew me into the pantry. The little room desperately needed to be cleaned out. Hanging off the edge of the top shelf was the green plastic derby and shamrock garland from last year's St. Paddy's Day party. We had a family celebration that included having my then-boyfriend, Mark, don his green blazer—the official Chamber of Commerce Ambassador coat—and the silly little derby. That romance had gone the way of last year's spring rains; it dried up and disappeared by July.

I put on the derby and draped the garland around my neck, then went on to clean out the small closet, clanking around and reorganizing things. I couldn't make order in my life, so I would make order there. It was a start.

I checked expiration dates on boxes and cans and began to accumulate a pile of food that I had to throw away. Good food gone to waste. It was only I in this house and I still shopped and stored goods as if I was going to feed an army. That would have to stop now. There wouldn't be money for it.

The lights flickered once, and then again, and finally went out. After finding a flashlight in the cupboard above the dryer, I stretched up to the pantry's top shelf searching for candles. I finally located several scattered about in different boxes. At work, I had been so proud of my organizational skills but my home was a wreck. I felt like such a failure.

With a sigh, I took the candles into the kitchen, pulled some candlesticks from the china cabinet, and set the candles around the room after lighting them. Then I fumbled with the phone book, looking for the number for the electric company's emergency hotline. I was told that it would be some time before anyone got around to fixing my lines. A benefit of living on the far edge of town nearly out in the country. There were neighbors on acreages around me, but the closest was about a block away. Most houses sat much farther back from the road than mine and were sheltered in the trees of the surrounding forest.

The rain continued to pound the earth, falling in torrents. Before the electricity had gone out I hadn't even turned on the television to see how long this storm was going to last or how bad it might be. I was too involved in thoughts of my not-so-bright future. I looked out the front windows and recalled that the road out to my house often flooded during heavy rain. One time the water had risen to within a few feet of the foundation. What if I got stuck at home, alone, and had to wait in the dark while the water crept across the yard? Maybe it would be better if I went into town and waited it out at the church. There were bound to be other people there, in the same fix that I was in. I could come home later when the storm had passed and the water had receded. I pitched the green hat and garland onto the table and grabbed a raincoat and umbrella.

I had driven only a hundred yards or so down the road toward town when I began to see the water rising to the tops of the bar ditches on either side. At the small bridge over Center Creek, the water was an inch or two over the road and over the surface of the bridge. It was racing along, but I could still see the bridge intact below the water.

I knew that it wasn't smart to drive into the flood, so I stopped my car and waited, wondering if I should try it. I slowly drove a little closer to the bridge and suddenly my car pitched nose-down several inches. The road had washed away on this end of the bridge! My car died and wouldn't start again.

Panicked, I watched the water rush over the bridge and beneath my car, my heart thumping. How long would it be before the water rises enough to pick my car up and float it down into the creek? The way the rain was falling, I was certain that it wouldn't be long. What should I do? Frantically, I looked out the driver's window at the water. Maybe I should climb over the seat and go out the back doors. Awkwardly, I slipped over the front seat and into the back, my purse and keys in one hand. I slung the shoulder bag around my neck, and then opened the back door. Filthy, brown water swirled just below the doorframe.

There was a shout and when I looked up, a man in a green slicker was waving at me from a forest service SUV parked just at the edge of the rushing water. He held a rope looped in one hand with a life preserver tied to one end.

Over the sound of the pouring rain and swirling water, the man shouted, "Grab the preserver and I'll pull you in!"

I reached out as far as I could to try to catch the rope as he threw it to the car. With his first throw the preserver came close enough that I could grab it. Slowly, I put one foot out into the rushing water. The force of the ankle-high water flowing under the car would've pulled me off balance if I didn't have the car to lean against and the preserver to hold on to. I planted my feet carefully and began to pull myself along the rope to the man. At the same time, he pulled the rope toward him. The water was now creeping up my shin. The process was slow. If I fell, I'd be washed away! Finally I was out of the deeper water and able to slosh toward him.

"You all right?"

"Yes." I looked up at his face. He was wearing a hat covered with a plastic cap as well as the green rain slicker. Compared to me he looked fairly dry and comfortable. My raincoat had done little to stand up to the downpour and I was completely soaked to the skin and shivering in the cold rain.

"Thank you so much!"

"You're welcome. You live around here?"

I pointed at my house, which was within sight just down the road.

"Hop in and I'll run you home."

I looked back at my car. Would it still be there when I had the chance to retrieve it? And there was one more problem. How would I ever find the money to repair the car, or get a new one? I had a $2,000 deductible on my car insurance. I gritted my teeth and got into his SUV.

"I'm Paul Novak," he said.

"Hello, Paul Novak. Emma Riordan." At least I couldn't chatter with my teeth gritted. What was I going to do about my car?

He began to back down the road, watching through the SUV's rear window, which was equipped with wipers.

"Two more houses. The gray one, there," I said as I turned to watch him maneuver down the rain-covered road. The back of the SUV was full of boxes, tools, ropes, and signs.

"You're with the forest service?" I asked. I didn't really care where he worked but the silence from the man who'd just rescued my poor excuse for a life was awkward. I ought to be thanking him over and over, but at that moment I was actually thinking that perhaps I should have stayed with the car and let the water wash both it and me down into the river.

67

He smiled. "Sort of. I work at the nature center down the road."

I took my grandchildren there the last time they had been here to visit for a weekend. It was a rustic place with a huge, stone fireplace and rooms filled with display cases and exhibits about trees, plants, and animals. My grandson, Dakota, had been fascinated with the insect display, while Skylar had cooed over the mammal exhibit and wanted to touch the stuffed skunks and raccoon. It had been a comfortable place, sort of like a combination of a rustic hotel and a museum. I pondered the fact that I lived in this area for twenty years and had never once taken the time to visit the center before. Time had passed me by. I spent my life working too hard at a place that offered me no loyalty whatsoever in the end.

I looked at Paul Novak as he drove. What kind of guy spent his life in a nature center? He was good looking, well groomed, well educated, and might be about my age. Still, he and I would have nothing in common to talk about. What was the use in trying? I looked out the front window of the car as he turned into the long driveway to my home at the edge of the trees.

I thanked him again. I didn't see the point of inviting him in to dry off and have a cup of hot tea. His cell phone rang and he waved at me, so I went into my house.

Nice man, I thought to myself. Way out of my league. Fat chance that an unemployed, overweight woman who doesn't have enough sense to stay out of the rain would be of any interest to him. I tried the light switch in the hallway. The power was still out.

I walked down the hallway in the semidarkness toward the kitchen and then stopped in the doorway. There, sitting on the island, was a squirrel holding something shiny in its little paws. The squirrel flicked its tail up and down, watching me with beady, black rodent eyes. Behind it, the French doors were still open a crack. Rain had blown in and the tile floor was wet. The animal had obviously come into the house through the French doors. Now, how was I going to get it out?

The squired chattered, startling me. I flinched and it leapt for the top of the refrigerator, scrambling through an assortment of bottles and an open bag of candy. The whole mess tumbled down and hit the floor, rolling with such a clatter that the squirrel freaked out even more. It leapt to the top of the cabinet and ran along the molding, knocking over knickknacks, ivy, and other collectibles that I had placed there. Finally, the frantic squirrel backed into the far corner of the kitchen, up close to the ceiling. It stared down at me.

How in the world do you get a frightened squirrel out of a house? I remembered reading somewhere that a squirrel is a rodent and I knew that rodents carry diseases. What was I going to do? I looked at the mess on the floor, including the cracked plates and cups that I'd kept from when the kids were little. It was all for naught now. What else was the animal going to destroy before I got it out of the house? I pictured the rest of the kitchen a shambles, with appliances on the floor and more dishes broken. What if the squirrel made it into the living room? There were more collectibles in there, all breakable. In minutes, the squirrel could be tearing across the room through the door and into the rest of the house. How was I going to get it out of there?

"Paul!" I ran for the front door. If anyone knew what to do with a squirrel it would be a naturalist. Paul had all those things in the back of his SUV. Surely there was a squirrel cage there, or something he could use to catch the animal.

He was still sitting in the driveway, talking on his cell. "Paul!" I screamed, waving my arms frantically until I caught his attention.

He got out of the car and dashed through the rain for the porch.

"Something wrong?"

"There's a squirrel in my kitchen! I don't know how to get it out of the house. Can you help?"

His face broke into a smile. "A squirrel? How did that happen?"

"I had the doors to the patio open earlier for fresh air and I forgot to latch them when I left. Stupid of me, but then I haven't been thinking straight lately." I didn't want to explain further. How could I tell him that I was a forgetful, unemployed accounting assistant? Leaving a door open during a storm wasn't smart.

He followed me through the house to the kitchen. The squirrel scolded us from its perch on the far kitchen cabinet.

"How do we get it down from there?" I asked.

Paul thought for a minute. "I'll run back out to the truck. I've got a fishnet out there; maybe I can scoop it into it and carry it outside."

He went back out to the truck in the rain and soon returned, armed with nets and bags and poles. Over the next thirty minutes, we struggled to trap the squirrel. When Paul moved at the feisty creature from one direction, the squirrel went the other way—always exactly where we didn't want it to go.

"You come at it from that way and I'll stand here," Paul finally instructed me. "Chase it toward the net." I did as I was told, and the squirrel dashed off right between us to the other side of the kitchen, racing once again up to the counter.

From there, the squirrel was closer to the French doors where it had come in. Paul decided we should open the doors all the way and see if the squirrel would run back outside. Sure enough, with one of us coming at it from each direction, the squirrel scampered down the side of the cabinets, across the kitchen floor, and out the doors.

We collapsed into the chairs at the kitchen table, laughing. The

69

kitchen was a disaster, with spilled salt on the counter and a canister of flour upended on the floor, not to mention broken dishes, pill bottles, and assorted colored candy.

"How about some tea or coffee?" I heard myself ask.

"Great!" Paul nodded. "Tea, then. And I'll start cleaning up this mess." He went to the sink, pulled off a handful of paper towels, and started to work.

I pulled out the teakettle and put it on the stove. What was I thinking? I had invited him to stay. I had nothing to say to him. We had nothing in common. This was going to be so awkward. The electric starter for the gas stove didn't work. I pulled out a match and lit the gas burner. Then I lit the candles on the counter that had survived the squirrel's adventure.

When I turned around, Paul had put on the St. Patrick's Day derby and draped the shamrock garland around his shoulders. He was whistling an Irish tune as he worked. I smiled and stopped to watch. He was a little large for a leprechaun but other than that, he looked and acted the part. The emerald green countryside could've been a spot in Ireland. Outside, the torrents had diminished into light rain. He caught my glance but kept right on dancing as he swept up the floor and wiped off the counters. I felt myself blush, something I hadn't done in years. Then I pulled off a few more paper towels and set to work as well, humming the tune he was whistling. It was one of my grandfather's favorites, "Rose of Killarney."

"Aye, 'tis fine to see a lass lettin' a laddie be o' help," Paul said in a terrible imitation of an Irish accent.

I laughed. "Aye, 'tis fine." I turned back to making the tea, ready to burst out laughing as I thought about the squirrel and this man in my candlelit kitchen.

"So, Emma, lass. You be havin' many encounters with squirrels during your housekeepin'?" His fake Irish accent continued.

"No." I laughed again. "Actually, I'm a sporadic housekeeper. Can't you tell?" Was he grading my housekeeping ability? What did he think of me?

"Ah, no. Looks grand t' me. I'm not much for housekeeping meself. Too many other things I be a-wantin' to do."

I set our mugs on the table with a couple of candlesticks and then sank down into one of the chairs. Paul took a seat and had a sip.

"Enough of that. Sorry for the accent. I'm Irish on my mother's side and today it just felt right. It is St. Paddy's day." He took off the garland and the plastic derby and laid them on the table between us.

"I know. I'm Irish, too." I smiled. Silence fell. We had nothing to talk about. He would be back out the door in five minutes.

"So, you're off today. Made it a holiday or do you work out of your home?" He smiled easily as he talked and his eyes were curious.

What should I tell him about me? The words tumbled out of my mouth before I made a conscious decision. "Actually, I'm just recently at home. Laid off after ten years. Don't exactly know what I'm going to do with myself next."

He looked up at me with interest. "So, what have you been doing for the past ten years?" The flickering candlelight reflected in his eyes made them twinkle.

"I'm a secretarial assistant in an accounting firm. Drafting letters, organizing client files, arranging meetings, and setting up conferences. The firm is outsourcing a lot of the accounting work and they no longer need me." I stared down into my mug, unable to look up at his face. He was surely looking at me with pity and getting ready to leave.

"I'm sorry you've had a stroke of bad luck," Paul said.

As I looked around the shadowy room, I thought to myself: A stroke of bad luck? A squirrel disaster, my car lost in the creek, and laid off all within twenty-four hours. If this is a stroke, I want to see a full-blown bout of bad luck.

A deep sigh slipped out from my lips and I felt my throat clench. I was going to cry right in front of this stranger. I was humiliated. Tears filled my eyes and spilled out over my cheeks.

His hand reached across the table to cover mine. "You've had a terrible couple of days, haven't you, Emma? I'm so sorry."

I got up and went to the sink to pull a few tissues from the box on the windowsill. I fully expected that Paul would get up to go when I turned my back to him, but when I turned around he was looking out at the forest, sipping his drink, not looking at all like he intended to leave. I sat back down at the table.

"Looks like the rain is easing up," he said.

I nodded and sniffed as I finished the last bit of tea.

"And you know things are bound to get better. In a little while, we'll take a drive back down the road and retrieve your car. I've got a wench on the front, and we'll drag it right back out of that hole and pull it home."

"That would be great, Paul. You're very kind. You don't even know me."

"Tell me what kind of things you did for your accounting firm."

I explained what a typical week was like and all the things that I did for the firm and its clients. He nodded as I spoke, as if he was truly interested in what I had to say.

"You know," he said when I had finished. "We have an opening at the nature center for a receptionist/secretary. You'd be perfect, if you're interested."

Startled, I nearly knocked over my empty mug. "At the nature center?" I stammered. "I don't know anything about nature. I've been in an office my whole life and I'm only living here at the edge of town because my husband loved this house and I couldn't bear to leave it after he died."

Paul nodded and looked down at his mug. Had I offended him?

"I just never thought about working at a place like that." I tried to explain, but everything I said sounded wrong. "I've been to the center and it's a great place. I can't imagine being able to work there and getting paid for it!" I remembered the wonderful feeling I had at the center when I visited it with my grandchildren. What would it be like to work there? "I don't know much about nature, though. I'm afraid I'd be of no help."

"You can learn, just like I did, if you want to. It can be very rewarding and there's always something new to learn about." When I didn't respond, he continued, "Well, it was just a thought. I realize it's a totally different work climate. Think about it. We'll talk about it again in another day or so."

He got up from the table and walked toward the front door. "Let's see what the water on the road is doing." We stepped out onto the front porch and there, in the sky across the road, hung a rainbow. He smiled and suddenly I felt lighter than I had in two days. "Look, I think the rain has let up enough that the water may be off the road. Let's sit just another minute or two, and then we'll go down and get your car."

He settled himself into the porch swing and I sat down beside him. We rocked, and as we rocked he told me stories about working at the nature center and how much he loved working with the children and adults that came there. He had an easy way of talking and laughed frequently. I mostly listened, still uncertain about what I was experiencing. Was this real? Had this man really come into my life and just offered me a job? Could I really be successful working in a totally different environment from what I was used to? Did I dare make that kind of change at this stage in my life?

Eventually, we drove down the road to my car and found that the water had receded from the pavement. The car was still there, tilted down into the section that had washed away. He attached a cable to the rear bumper as I slipped into my car and put it in neutral, then he dragged it backward with his SUV until it was flat again on the road. I steered as he pulled my car home, and all the way up the driveway.

Paul Novak got out of his SUV and walked up to the porch with me, holding his U.S. Forest Service hat in his hands. "You'll think about the job, Emma? I really am serious. I'll call you in a few days to talk with you about it. Come by the center before then, if you'd like. I'll give you the tour."

As his SUV backed down the driveway, I stared after him from the porch. He was a nice man and I needed a job. The nature center was only a few miles away. What would it be like to work there? I always told myself that I had to stay within the accounting profession. After all, it was what I had done for years. Would it really be possible for me to try something different?

I went back into the kitchen. There on the table was the green plastic derby and the shamrock garland. I felt like whistling. It felt like my burden had been lifted. I hadn't yet made up my mind what I wanted to do, but I knew that there were possibilities out there. What I really needed was to get out and find out what they were and to start living again. Paul just might have been my own personal St. Paddy's Day leprechaun.

I glanced out the French doors to the patio and saw the squirrel, perched on the patio table. It looked at me and flicked its tail. The sun had come out.

THE END

# IRISH IN AMERICA
## A St. Patrick's Day Love Story

$M$any things are put off until the time is right in this fast-paced world we live in. But what makes the time right? Where will life lead us and how do we know we're headed in the right direction?

My niece, Kelly, and Kevin, her boyfriend, were just one couple out of many who wanted to know if they'd be doing the right thing by getting married.

They each carried the been-there-done-that-won't-do-it-again attitude from their previous marriage with children to raise and daily living events to deal with. Yet these things were just what lead them to the world's biggest shamrock listed in the Guinness Book of World Records.

Kelly and Kevin grew up in the small, Irish mid-western town of O'Neill, Nebraska. Kevin was the first baby born on St. Patrick's Day the year O'Neill held its very first St. Patrick's Day celebration. He grew into a tall, brawny lad two years older than Kelly. He was in the same grade as her only brother, Mike, and Mike and Kevin were best friends. Kevin spent a lot of time at Mike's house and at that time Kelly was thought of as Mike's baby sister, a pest that had to be tolerated.

Kelly was always on the short side and was never taken to be as old as she was or taken very seriously. In her junior high years, Kelly faced life with her own mindset. In her teen years, she saw Kevin in a different light, which turned into a teenage crush. Unfortunately, Kevin quit school, moved away, and later got married. Kelly finished high school in O'Neill and then was off to further her education in a town three hundred miles away. There she met a guy her own age, got married, and had a son. Kelly and Kevin each traveled in different directions down life's road but ended up in the same situation: divorced with children.

Kelly moved back to O'Neill to be by her folks. When Kelly and Kevin's paths crossed again, Kevin had come to visit O'Neill and both were at the same bar. Kevin was standing against a wall when Kelly spotted him. Her heart gave a leap at the sight of him and thoughts of I don't believe it! raced through her mind as she approached him.

"Hi, Kevin. Do you remember me? I'm Kelly, Mike's sister?

"Yeah, I know you."

With no more encouragement and figuring Kevin wasn't interested in her, Kelly returned to her seat. Kevin's thoughts turned to the years before either of them had been married. He knew that Kelly had a crush on him back then and he knew life might have turned out differently if he hadn't moved away. He kept an eye on her for a while and when the band played a slow tune, he got up enough courage to walk over to where she was sitting and asked her to dance. As they danced and talked, Kevin let his guard down and began opening up to Kelly.

"I'm divorced and I have three children. I'm only here on a visit but if you'll let me see you, I'll try to come back every other weekend."

As old feelings crept in on Kelly, she became putty in his hands and she agreed to the arrangement.

Eventually, Kevin moved back to O'Neill and became a twosome with Kelly. As their lives became entwined, Kevin knew that he loved Kelly and didn't want to lose her. The first time Kevin asked Kelly to marry him, she responded with, "Been there, done that, won't do it again."

Kevin knew that he wasn't about to give up that easily. With Kevin spending more and more time with Kelly at her parents' home, Kelly's father began adding his two cent's worth in favor of a marriage and promised Kevin a hundred dollars if he could get Kelly to say yes.

Each time the subject was brought up, Kelly's response was, "The time isn't right." One year passed, then another. Kelly and Kevin joked about getting married and Kelly's father would ante-up his promise of another hundred dollars if only Kevin could get Kelly to marry him. In time the couple thought they would get married, only they wanted each of their children to be okay with the marriage and be part of the decision when they did get married.

As time and fate would have it, Kelly and Kevin began sharing an apartment, facing whatever life had in store. The first major catastrophe they faced together was when Kevin had a car accident and then again after he took a roofing job with his cousins. While on the roofing job he stood up, stepped backward to survey what had been accomplished, and fell three stories down through a ten-foot opening left by the contractors working on the building. This put Kevin in the hospital for almost six months and he needed back surgery. It would be three years before he could work again, yet Kelly stayed by his side.

But then Kelly's mom was diagnosed with a brain tumor and the long trips to Omaha for treatment began, and then follow-up checkups. Kelly's father's ante-up marriage offer kept going up, but still the time wasn't right. By the time Kelly's mother reached the five-year mark to be declared cancer-free, the cancer had returned to a different place in her body. The cancer that reappeared as a tumor in her stomach area had already gotten to the point where little could be done. A month later, on her deathbed, she mentioned wishes for Kelly and Kevin to get married. Kelly's promise of "When the time is right" became "We will."

Kelly and Kevin's attention became centered on their needs, as well as Kelly's father's needs. The company Kelly's dad had worked at for almost twenty years as an auto body repairman was closing their doors and filing for bankruptcy. At his age and with an eighth grade education, he had little prospects of landing a good job. It was his job that took the family away from the rest of the relatives. Feeling the need and wanting to be closer to the family again when job openings came up, Kevin and Kelly made the move closer to family with hopes of her dad moving, too. Instead, five months after Kelly's mother died, her fifty-nine-year-old father died of an unexpected heart attack. Families draw closer when sharing losses. I lost my brother and I knew that he'd want me to be there for his daughter. I tried to be there, along with Kevin and others. The question of What's next? hung in all our minds.

It was just before Christmas at our family's get-together that things started falling into play.

Kelly announced the official news: "Kevin and I are going to get married. No date yet, but when the time is right we'll let you know,"

A month passed before we received a special e-mail:

Hi everyone! Just wanted to let you know what Kevin and I are trying to work out for a wedding. A radio station is hosting the Hottest Wedding. On Valentine's Day, they'll marry one couple on the air. They get the bride her gown and the groom his tux, plus others who would walk out to the parking lot, strip down to their swim suits, and get married in a hot tub. They're taking e-mail nominations for a week. I think after nine going on ten years of being together, this would be the "something" we need to give us the little kick to get things done!

That morning found those interested in the Hottest Wedding glued to the radio as the five couples' names were revealed. It seemed the time might be right—the time that Kelly and Kevin thought would never come—when their names were among couples chosen. The feeling that this might be the kind of wedding that could make a dream come true for the fun-loving couple was shared by most of the family. The following week, a "Pre-Newlywed Game" started. Each day for the next five days, one of the couples was interviewed, asked questions, and scored on their answers. After the interviews, two couples were to be chosen and the public would pick the winner. Every family member that had access to a radio had it tuned to the Pre-Newlywed Game.

At the end of the day, Kelly wrote an e-mail message and sent it to keep us up-to-date with what was going on. Kelly and Kevin were interviewed on the second day and scored the highest points right from the start. By the end of the five days, two couples shared second place. So it was decided that there would be three couples' names to be voted on and the game advanced to voting by the public. Phone votes were taken from eight o'clock until ten-thirty in the mornings and via e-mail votes from eight in the morning until midnight. This caused the first glitch. One vote on a computer locked that computer out, voters who would've shared a computer couldn't get through with a phone vote, and yet some voters knew how to reset a computer to really tally up the votes. Neither way of voting turned out fair.

Trying to correct that mistake, each couples' name was listed together on a piece of paper and put in a hat. The couples' name on the piece of paper drawn out would be considered the winner of the contest. Kelly and Kevin's names were not the names drawn. The names of the couple that was drawn were not even listed as one in the play-off game. To top everything off, the Hottest Wedding took a turn for the worst when a freak ice storm landed during the night of the thirteenth. People couldn't travel. The ice turned to rain, then snow. The wedding went on as planned, only in freezing weather with very few people able to attend. With the way everything turned out, it just wasn't the right time for Kelly and Kevin to get married. Even though the first attempt to find the right time had turned cold and very disappointing, Kelly was not ready to give up on finding a way to make their wedding one to remember.

Kevin's thirty-fifth birthday was coming up on O'Neill's annual St. Patrick's Day celebration, which Kelly and Kevin took part in many times in past years. With that in mind, Kelly's heart began to beat not only a birthday tune but also a wedding march. The idea of being the first couple married on the world's biggest shamrock listed in the Guinness Book of World Records during the town's St. Patrick's Day celebration took hold. Kelly was sure that the time was right, the place would be perfect, and set about to make her dream come true. Kelly felt it was appropriate; the first baby born on St. Patrick's Day the year of the town's first celebration will be the first groom married on the town's shamrock!

Kelly began to make the necessary calls to receive permission to hold her wedding during the celebration. Kevin works as a youth counselor at the Springfield Academy Correctional Center for boys. With permission granted, Reverend McMann, who also worked with the boys at the center, agreed to officiate at the wedding.

The town newspaper announced the upcoming wedding plans that were to take place in the middle of the big shamrock after the Irish step dancers performed at noon and the presentation of the Irish king and queen. On a bright, sunny day, and with the luck of the Irish on St. Patrick's Day, Kelly and Kevin exchanged wedding vows; Kelly, in her long, green wedding gown, carrying a bouquet of green-and-white carnations with sprays of shamrocks and Kevin, wearing a shamrock vest, white shirt and tie with black pants. Beside them in the middle of the famous shamrock also stood Kelly's cousin as her bridesmaid, in a green dress; Kevin's brother for his best man, in attire matching Kevin's; and Kelly's son as ring barer. Family members, friends, and thousands of other people witnessed the ceremony. At the close of the ceremony, the band played the wedding march and the couple was lead away to become part of the St. Patrick's Day parade. The "glitch" did turn into a hitch on a beautiful day—when the time was right. One could bet a much-loved couple in heaven was watching the festivities with a smile on their faces—and Kelly's dad could rest in peace knowing that Kevin wasn't really after the ante-up money.

THE END

# WHEN IRISH EYES ARE SMILING...
## People Fall In Love!

I looked up at the sign of the pub as I gathered my courage and opened the door. My friend, Rick, had told me to meet him at Connolly's. Now, there I was, wearing a pretty dress and wondering if he'd make it. The only reason I'd agreed to meet him was so I wouldn't have to spend St. Patrick's Day alone. No person of Irish descent should have to do that!

I walked into the noisy pub and looked around. No Rick. With my luck he won't show at all. I turned around and bumped right into the epitome of a tall, dark, and handsome man.

"Whoa," he said in a deep, sexy voice. He jumped out of my way. "Going somewhere?"

I looked up into his absolutely gorgeous eyes. "Excuse me," I said, my eyes traveling down his hunky body. I turned red as a beet when I realized that I'd made him spill his drink.

"Oh, I'm so sorry."

"No problem, I can always get another drink. Are you really leaving? The party is just beginning. Why don't you come on back in?"

"I was supposed to meet someone but I don't see him anywhere."

"Well, let me get you a drink and of course a green party hat to match and that oh-so-Irish hair."

I followed his incredible build with an interested stare. He came back and handed me the drink and stuck the silly little hat on my head.

"Thanks," I managed, and blushed hotly as his gaze raked over my low-cut, white dress.

"Have you seen your friend?" he asked, his eyes twinkling.

I glanced around the pub. "Nope, no sign of him."

"His loss. I'm Steve Shannahan. Would you join me at my table?"

"Colleen Doyle, and lead the way."

He laughed. "At least we have nice, respectable, Irish names. And no Irish woman should spend the holiday alone! Not one as pretty as you, anyway," he said.

"I said that same thing to myself when I came in." I put my hand through his arm as he headed to his table.

The band in the corner tuned up and the band leader came to the mike. "Folks, we'll have all kinds of dancing music tonight, but our first number will be a good, old Irish reel. We'll see how many of you are truly Irish!"

79

Steve grinned at me and held out his hand. "Come, my little Irish maid. We'll show these people what the jig is all about!"

I grinned back, took his hand, and asked, "And just how do you know I can do this?"

He pulled me to him. "It doesn't matter whether you can or not. It's just an excuse to get you closer." His husky voice breathed into my ear and made the delicious chills start again.

I smiled up at him and took a deep breath. The scent of his aftershave curled around my head, giving me an intoxicating rush.

"Well, you're just lucky my granny taught me this," I said, and launched into a perfect jig.

Steve raised his eyebrows and joined me. We danced around the whole floor to the applause of the rest of the crowd.

"Granny taught you well, I see," Steve said afterward as he led me back to the table.

"She always said I was part leprechaun."

Steve leaned down and kissed me before he let me go. I felt it to my toes. Without thinking, I returned the kiss. Everyone was still clapping over the dance and they all really hooted at this scene. We were oblivious to the yelling.

"I never kissed a leprechaun before," he whispered breathlessly into my ear.

"Is it any different from kissing a regular girl?"

"Oh, much better. Much better." He pulled my chair out and I sat down, still reeling from the kiss.

"I think I'll get us some fresh drinks. Don't go away, he teased. He ran his fingers down my cheek in a sensual caress.

When he came back, the band was playing a soft, slow song and Steve again pulled me from my chair.

"Let's try some regular dancing." He gathered me close and we swayed with expertise to the music.

I leaned against his strong chest and sighed. And just think, I thought I might have to spend St. Patrick's Day alone!

Steve reached under my chin, lifted my face up, and kissed me again. I could almost see the sparks flying around my head.

"What if your friend shows up?" Steve asked, his breath moving my curls.

"What friend? Oh, yes. That friend. We'll just have the bartender tell him I left in search of my pot of gold."

Steve laughed and held me closer. "I think a beautiful leprechaun led me to my pot of gold."

I melted into his embrace again and returned his kiss.

THE END